About the Author

Katrina Morrow studied cinema and journalism at the City College of San Francisco and she currently lives in Santa Cruz where she practices writing for social justice causes.

The Reverse Fate of the Challenger

Katrina Morrow

The Reverse Fate of the Challenger

Olympia Publishers
London

www.olympiapublishers.com
OLYMPIA PAPERBACK EDITION

A CIP catalogue record for this title is
available from the British Library.

ISBN: 978-1-80439-442-7

This is a work of fiction.
Names, characters, places and incidents originate from the writer's
imagination. Any resemblance to actual persons, living or dead, is
purely coincidental.

First Published in 2023

Olympia Publishers
Tallis House
2 Tallis Street
London
EC4Y 0AB

Printed in Great Britain

Dedication

I dedicate this book to my great grandmother, Dorothy Young. What was taken hopefully and yet surely the Universe will accept back although despite it all I think the world should be flooded with everybody's own personal Challenger story.

Preface

Astronaut of the Challenger, Ronald McNair, no doubt had his term paper for his doctorate stolen from him while studying at MIT. This was a setback for him while he was in school but he was able to produce another PHD physics research paper and was able to then graduate with a physics degree in 1976. What happened to McNair is actually pretty common as to when white folks steal the creative ideas of black folks without giving them credit for the original idea. In this novel I demonstrate this recurring phenomenon of white culture stealing from African Americans, for it is the basis of this story. It is a form of cultural appropriation, but it goes beyond even that as the thefts take place just to maintain white supremacy culture. In this novel I have fictionalized Ronald McNair's story and I have amended the story to my own experiences of creative thievery as a black woman myself but passing for white. One of the greatest creative thefts in history of stealing from black folks is the song "The Lion Sleeps Tonight" originally created by Solomon Linda of Africa but corporate companies like Disney stole the song and didn't share the profits with Linda (The Root). And Picasso stole the artistic ideas of Africans, and art historians said it was both theft and cultural appropriation. And the South African Department of the Arts and Culture spokesperson Sandile Memela said this of Picasso's work at an African exhibit: "Today the truth is on display that Picasso would not have been the renowned creative genius he was if he did not steal and re-adapt the work of anonymous African artists" (The Root).

Another major theft in black creative history is when the American band Led Zeppelin was sued by Willie Dixon of Muddy Waters for stealing his guitar scores. The creative theft case was eventually settled out of court (The Root). And there was vaudeville comedian Charlie Chase whose songs and other material were stolen by white comedians who performed his creative ideas in front of white audiences in the 1920s (The Root). Perhaps one of the more complicated creative thefts against blacks is Willie Mae Thornton's "Hound Dog" song. While Thornton recorded the song in August of 1952, it became a popular hit so he immediately filed a copyright for the song. However, several artists subsequently started to steal the song anyway. First Freddie Bell and the Bellboys stole it from Little Esther – who took it from the original source which was Thornton but then Elvis Presley made the song famous for himself in which he took it from the Bellboys. But the "Hound Dog" song was eventually credited to the white men who had paid for the recording of the song (The Root).

The other dynamic in this story is the historical phrase of "passing" when a person of both white and black heritages passes for white and seemingly escapes the persecutions of being black because they look white. This is the case in my own personal life story, which I have outlined in the novel. While most of the time people identify me as being white, once in a blue moon someone will come up to me and tell me that they know that I am a black woman. I remember in the early 2000s when I was still in my twenties a black man came up to me in San Francisco's Hayes valley and looked me straight in the eye and said "you are a black woman". And I asked him how he knew this and replied to me that he's been "around a long time". Most of the time I consider myself not so lucky as to when most people identify me as being white. This has been the greatest pain of my life because I would love for people to see my black side, in which there is much power in being black. Although I am not the only one who writes and passes for white. There was Charles W. Chesnutt before me who wrote books about the phenomenon of "passing" in the post-Civil War South. Before he wrote *The House Behind the Cedars* he said this: "I think I must write a book. It has been my cherished dream and I feel an influence that I cannot resist calling to the task." His novel *The House Behind the Cedars* is about love and relationships and passing for white at the same time. However, because the story is set in the post-Civil War South, tension arises when the one who is "passing" is found out of their black side by their lover. Charles W. Chesnutt has said this of the human heart: "The workings of the human heart are the most profound mystery of the universe. One moment they make us despair of our kind and the next we see in them the reflection of the divine image." Charles W. Chesnutt was of the Antebellum era but soon after there was a Broadway actress named Carol Channing who also was mixed with both black and white but like Chesnutt she passed for white. She said this of the matter when her mother told her about her black grandmother when she was sixteen: "I was sixteen years old and my mother told me, and you know, only the reaction on me was, Gee I got the greatest genes in show business." Carol Channing's career as an actress spanned from the 1940s to 2017 in which in the early 2000s she publicly announced that she was a black woman but "passing" all the years before.

Introduction

Temperatures on the morning the space shuttle the Challenger took off were below freezing. And spacecraft engineers were concerned that O-ring rubber seals in the solid rocket boosters would distress in the very low temperatures. And, despite their warnings, the Challenger took off at 11.38 a.m. on the morning of January 28, 1986 but then exploded in mid-air seventy-three seconds into its flight. This was actually the space shuttle's tenth mission and it had completed space missions in the past. Not only had it completed a mission where an astronaut repaired a satellite in April of 1984, the shuttle had seen a cultural diversity among its cabinet – the first woman, named Sally Ride, rode the Challenger on space mission STS-7 of June 1983. And the first black astronaut, named Guion Bluford, also rode the Challenger on flight STS-8. Also the spacecraft launched into space successfully on April 4, 1983 on mission STS-6 with astronauts Story Musgrave and Donald Peterson who both completed the first spacewalk of the Shuttle program. And, despite the mission failure of 1986, this space shuttle completed nine missions with a total of three years of service. The total space hours of this spacecraft is sixty-two days, seven hours, fifty-six minutes and twenty-two seconds. Moreover, this space shuttle was the first spacewalk of April 7, 1983. And according to the Kennedy Space Center the shuttle was to be just a test vehicle – the shuttle was first sent to Rockwell International aerospace manufacturing company and then sent to Lockheed Martin for testing on April

2, 1978 (reference for business). At this time NASA claims that computers for measuring stresses on the shuttle were not equipped enough to understand stressors at different times of flight. Furthermore, NASA claims the shuttle went through eleven months of vibration testing. During the second test NASA found cracks in the main engine were causing leaks. And there was something wrong with the three hydraulic cylinders which were at one million lbs. of force and a substitute for the main engines. Later, in 1979, NASA granted Rockwell International to test the shuttle into an actual spacecraft and on October 23, 1981 the work was completed (NASA). The shuttle was supposed to launch into space on Jan 20 1983 but NASA found a hydrogen leak in the main engine (science.ksc.) (space.com).

Space shuttles are made of materials like porous silicon, which is very light and heat resistant (nasa.gov.), and the space shuttle is covered in LI-900 silica tiles made from pure quartz and sand (wikipedia.org). All the while the inner insulation prevents heat from getting into the orbiter which would be an aluminum surface and structure per se (wikipedia.org). Space shuttles are also made of light weight alloys of titanium, aluminum, and magnesium. Furthermore the aluminum is for the hydrazine and nitrous oxide propellant tank (astronomycafe.net). Moreover, aluminum is important for the making of a spacecraft because it is lightweight, but when combined with other materials it strengthens (azom.com). While space shuttles are made of materials like porous silicon and aluminum they also consist of three major components: first there is the winged orbiter that carries both the crew and cargo. Secondly there is the external tank with liquid hydrogen otherwise known as fuel and liquid oxygen for the orbiter's three main rocket engines. And solid propellant is strapped on large booster rockets (Britannica).

Lastly, space shuttles are powered by fuel cells which are a component of the electrical system. There are also three fuel cell power plants that experience a chemical reaction which will then generate the power needed for both launching and landing (nasa.gov).

The Justice Department came up with the conclusion that the rocket manufacturer was to blame for the disaster of the Challenger (NYTimes). It was determined that the crew may have been alive for at least ten seconds after the explosion, but both the spacecraft and the crew died by the impact onto the ocean (LA times, Wikipedia). Subsequently, four of the families of four astronauts received compensation from the federal government with 7.7 million dollars. As for the remains of the crew, they were found in the cabin and by the time NASA closed its investigation the spacecraft remained in the Atlantic Ocean (history.com). But of course, all the crew on board the fateful Challenger, their lives matter even to this day because they were on a space mission to encourage the education of space to the rest of the public.

The first crew member was not actually an astronaut but a public school teacher who was selected in an applicant pool of 11, 500 applicants of teachers who wanted to go on the space mission. Around 1984, former President Ronald Reagan and NASA made an announcement that they created the teacher in space program and Challenger crew member and teacher Christa McAuliffe won the contest, beating the 11,000 candidates. And at the White House, George H. W. Bush congratulated McAuliffe and said of her "the first private citizen passenger in the history of space flight". And in 1985 Christa McAuliffe went on intensive training at the Johnson Space Center in Houston Texas, and only returned home for the holidays. Christa McAuliffe was

15

born Sept 2, 1948 in Boston. She went to Framingham State College and studied American History and education and received her bachelor's degree in 1970. Subsequently she taught American history and English to junior high school students in Maryland. She was married to a former NASA space teacher candidate, Steve McAuliffe. To this day he is the founding director of the Challenger Center and he serves as a federal judge. Christa McAuliffe, although her life still matters, is buried at Blossom Hill Cemetery in NH (biography.com).

The Challenger had only one African American onboard when it took off and then dissipated in mid-air on the morning of January 28, 1986. Ronald McNair was the second African American to reach space in a former successful launch in February of 1984, alongside Guion Bluford. McNair became his successor when launching into space on the Challenger for the first time on mission STS-41-B. McNair operated the Challenger's robotic arm to assist then astronaut Bruce McCandless in his spacewalk. Ronald McNair was born in October of 1950 in South Carolina. His interest in space peaked at the age of seven when the Russian satellite first launched in 1957. He then went on to graduate high school as a valedictorian in 1967, and then graduated magna cum laude in 1971 with a BS in physics from the North Carolina Agricultural and technical State University. Subsequently upon college graduation he received a Ford Foundation fellowship to MIT. While at MIT he had a setback when his physics research paper for his doctorate was stolen, but he was able to produce a second one and then graduated with a PHD in physics in 1976. While he was a physicist at Hughes Research Laboratories he became aware of NASA's hunt for scientists for the space shuttle program. And out of 11,000 applicants, McNair was one of thirty-five chosen. He completed training for the shuttle program the following August. And, despite the fate of the Challenger, while McNair was onboard he actually completed a total of a hundred and ninety-one hours in space as the Challenger orbited the Earth a hundred and twenty-two times (biography.com).

The Challenger's pilot, Michael J. Smith, was the last voice recorded when he said to the mission control "go to throttle up". The Challenger of January 1986 was Michael Smith's first mission to space. He was born April 30, 1945 in North Carolina. He first learned to fly in aviation as a teenager. He received a bachelor's degree in Naval Science from the US Naval Academy and then a master's degree in Aeronautical engineering. From there he worked as a Navy pilot and then served in Vietnam. After he got his master's degree in Aeronautical engineering he went on to train as a naval aviator and then became a flight teacher. After a stint as a flight instructor he applied to the NASA astronaut program and was selected in 1980. He was then assigned pilot onboard STS-51-L, the Challenger (thoughtco).

Also onboard the famous Challenger was America's first Japanese American astronaut named Ellison S. Onizuka. He was born in Kona Hawaii on June 24th 1946. He graduated from high school with honors in 1964. He went on to attend the University of Colorado and obtained a bachelor of science in aeronautical engineering in 1968 and the following year he also obtained a masters in aeronautical engineering. Soon afterwards, he joined the Air Force in January of 1970 and attended the Air Force test pilot school of Edwards Air Force Base in August of 1974. And then he was up against 8,000 applicants for NASA's space shuttle program and was selected as one of thirty-five astronauts in 1978. And to repeat, this made him the first Japanese American astronaut in America's space program. His first successful space flight was onboard the Discovery, the country's first classified military space flight. And like all the other Challenger crew, his life mattered, as he once said: "your vision is not limited by what your eyes can see, but by what your mind can imagine. Make your life count and the world will be a better place because you tried."

(Astronaut Ellison S. Onizuka Memorial.)

The second female aboard the Challenger was Dr. Judith Resnick who was also the second female after Sally Ride to orbit in space. And before the ill-fated event of the Challenger, Resnick had already completed a total of a hundred and forty-four hours and fifty-seven minutes in space on the Discovery. She was born April 5, 1949 in Akron Ohio. She went on to become her high school's valedictorian. Initially, she wanted to become a concert pianist and was accepted at the Juilliard School of Music, but turned it down to study mathematics at Carnegie Mellon University where she also studied electrical engineering. She did her master's work at the University of Maryland and got her PHD in 1977. Subsequently she then worked at RCA on missile and radar programs for the military and research on integrated circuitry helped get her into NASA's astronaut program. While she was doing her graduate studies, she was accepted and qualified as an aircraft pilot, piloting for NASA's T-38 Talon aircraft. Finally in 1978 she became an astronaut and was one of six women to do so. She was the second American to fly and she followed the first woman in space, who was Sally Ride. Resnick gave credit to *Star Trek*'s actress Nichelle Nichols as her inspiration to want to fly to space. In addition to her lifelong accomplishments, schools are named after her and a lunar crater on the far side of the moon is called "Resnick" (thoughtco).

Gregory Jarvis was Challenger's other "payload specialist"

that also oversaw the study of weightlessness on fluids in space. He was born August 24, 1944 in Detroit Michigan. He obtained a BS in electrical engineering from the State University of New York and an MS in electrical engineering from Northeastern University. After school he was in the Air Force for four years and obtained the rank of captain. Soon after he worked for Hughes Aircraft from 1973–1984 where he worked as an engineer on satellite programs. He then worked for the MARISAT program on maritime communications satellites. He then went on to work for the military in communications systems. And in 1984 he, alongside his engineer colleagues at Hughes Aircraft, applied for payload specialist for NASA. He was then set to fly to space in 1985 but was replaced by both senators Jake Garn and Bill Nelson who wanted to fly to space as well. He was finally set to fly to space as payload specialist on the Challenger and his tasks included studying fluids in space and effects on liquid fueled rockets as part of fluid dynamics experiments. He also had duties that entailed testing the reaction of satellite propellants to shuttle maneuvers. After his death he was awarded the Congressional Space medal of Honor and an engineering building at the State University of New York is named after him as well as a dam in the state of New York (thoughtco).

Finally and last but not least is the Challenger's commander, Francis Scobee. He was born May 19, 1939 in Cle Elum Washington. After high school he enlisted in the United States Air Force and trained as a reciprocating engine mechanic. He went on to get a bachelor's in aerospace engineering from the University of Arizona. He then went to USAF Aerospace Research Pilot School at Edwards Air Force Base California in 1972. From here he became a test pilot in a series of test programs. As an Air Force test pilot he logged in more than 6,500 hours of flying time. Soon thereafter he became Lt. Col. Scobee in Vietnam; and also as a pilot while in Vietnam he was awarded the Distinguished Flying Cross and the Air Medal. He was a test pilot before he became an astronaut for NASA in 1978. In all actuality he was aboard the successful Challenger flight STS 41-C in 1984 that repaired and deployed a damaged satellite known as the Solar Maximum. Lastly, he was commander of the ill-fated Challenger where his life was taken but like the rest in the above, his life surely did matter as a public servant (amfcse.org).

Epigraph

Ode to the Challenger

Earth's sky opened up as you throttled upward and fateful hands like gravity must have turned on you. But fear not, because beings in space have a different plan for you for they have been waiting for you for the trillions of years called space. They plan to alter your fate so the stars stop crying at your tarot card calling. You are the pounds of aluminum so lightweight but the pull in space will hold you up. The crisp morning you are to take off will not scare the clouds as they wait for you to pass them by. And the morning crow with its deep chirping will fly with you as you go up into Earth's sky. God will also sit and wait for you for he is calling. As with the rest of the gods in what we call space will use the sun to guide you. If you shall not make it through the light in space will surely shake with tears like volcanic rage. The stars will spill their fire, but surely there is something else in it for you. For centuries space has been preparing for you and Earth's moon sees to it that you are its obedient child. You will not go down in history as a failure or a demise but as a star among all stars that sit in space like glory. You were tested and tested again and your character did not falter at their challenge. They did not want to retire you, despite your malfunctioning history, because you are the dear Challenger so close to the hearts of Americans. They too are waiting for you no matter how many years long it takes to get you back and grounded in a smooth sailing landing. Love is also waiting in the atmosphere as you fly up and love is the people you serve as you touch base with the moon. Let nothing ever stop you again for you are on a mission and a mission that shall never end for the truth is always calling. And the Atlantic Ocean will not be your tomb but your support as you fly above it. The ocean too would like to see you float in space like there was never any gravity to hold you back. The water will be like a compass within you and not an undertaker. The water blesses you, as water blesses all life even if you are buried there beneath its watery surface. Even if you crashed there all life recycles through the force of water. Your power will unite with the water's power and surely life will begin again. Although space would like to present a different plan for you, as you grow in your flight upwardly. Your shuttle wings at your side are as graceful as any bird in its flight. Rest assured though, that you are the crows' and the eagles' strength as they take note of you as you go up into your flight. And the wind will not bother you even if it is cold and freezing beyond belief toward your mission. For the winter in Florida is forgiving even if it is an early chilled morning – something of the southern warmth has got to give. Give you strength amidst the winter mourning of your launch. The circumstances should be held accountable for what happened to you, but anyways you still live in the imaginations of the youth of 1986. Don't ever again let space see you on your knees, for space will never again let you beg. And you are a vehicle of much grace and space is at your service to repair your soul and your honest spirit and intentions. If one could rewrite history they would surely write of your winged flight as a success. Even in death you are the most glorious space shuttle that ever launched off its base. And humanity wishes you the best as you lay to rest in the sea of much profound prophecy and legend. And you have become America's most darling legend and America is at your beck and call and not the other way around. The stars and the light in space will weep no more for they are smiling at your powerful tomb beneath great waters. You live like a great ancient queen that has already seen space at its bang. You didn't need to prove that you have seen the Universe for you have already been there nine times before. Dear Challenger, know that they did not want to retire you, for you were America's most prominent star as you have had a history of orbiting Earth and you were not at large when you did so. No man's hand could take you down like gravity would, no man's hands could murder your bright soul for you are the legendary Challenger. You fought with a sword with a velvet handle, whoever did this to you, but what they don't know is that you still serve humanity in your bravery and keen intention. Also know that the planets are lining up for you. They are waiting for the day you rise up from the ocean.

This author here believes that they should have retired you but you are now in the hall of martyrdom. Even as the life giving forces of the water that now surrounds you was hoping they would expire your flight future for your own life that now is in the depths of the kingdom of the ocean. But you are not dying, you are alive with your fame and your wake and your doom. Don't let the damn situation tell you otherwise; you are the Great Challenger that people still have in mind. It's not a case of out of sight out of mind, it is a case of history bound by the memory of you. The whales in the ocean sing your name as they pass by you for you are welcome in their place they call home. The sky never wanted to betray you, it just wanted to help you but someone or something got away with the demise of you. Don't let your grave become your mark, it is your flight history that has made the sacrifice. And if there are beings in space they would have

23

changed your fate, for the blessings of the Universe give life. And they would have tried to save you even considering the circumstances at the line between life and death. But this author here has altered your story for the better of humanity and your very shuttle. This author was just a child when you were taken but now an adult who can amend your story. And for the better and not to gain for the sake of your popularity will grow anyway. And it is in the opinion of this author that they should have flown you through the skies as a retiring space chief and ended your journey based on the fact of your repairs history. They should have done it based on their intelligence but they did not for reasons unknown even to humanity. It sure probably was because you are the Challenger that has seen the world of space already. And they believed in you with good intention; that is why they took a risk but you had to fall anyway but you're here in the hearts of Americans. And now angels sing your name like a Christmas carol for they know you are in the same martyrdom kingdom as they are. May the winds bless your story and carry it world-wide. For even as you rest you don't play their game and Africa and Japan are humming your name among the two continents so wide. And the astronauts' mausoleums stand so firm and so strong they are not going to try to alter what happened for they are in history's great kingdom. Their very graves mark their words that are like life giving stories to tell that would not otherwise be told. But mark these words: their lives mattered even as the impact on the ocean was just as powerful as each and every one of their names. And space was waiting for the Challenger and its astronauts and space is still waiting and the solar winds and the stars will never stop crying in their absence. You, dear Challenger, are the martyr so go forward with your story you are not alone for this author here will pay it forward to you and to humanity. And you are the gatekeeper of greatness, you are the ring bearer between space and humanity and you hold the key to what should have been. The rising tides of the oceans are speaking on your behalf and even the ocean did not compromise when you landed there. The ocean is not angry even though it should be, it gladly holds you in its arms and now only humanity is crying. But fear not, your fate is pending at the story of reversal and this author here is going to bring you justice. Justice for all of space and humans alike and justice for you, dear Challenger, for you are deserving of it. While the angels sing they also hold you up, up out of the ocean's depths you will fly up to meet your justice and your sweet wake and justified revenge.

Prologue

As hot fog curls up off of Jupiter the Alien Queen's monarch in space sits quiet and still. It is like a peaceful utopia that Jupiter is after so much pain from its past. The Alien Queen was born Aluna Grace to an alien mother and father who owned a spacecraft factory called "Space Shuttle and Space Ship Company" on planet Jupiter. After the history of Jupiter has seen its share of both peace and conflict, the planet was now in a state of alien utopia of a foundation laid down for centuries of peace and the helping of planet Earth. The Alien Queen had inherited the alien monarchy on Jupiter via her parents before her. It was a life giving and socialistic monarchy that was placed on Jupiter for many centuries after centuries of conflict. And the Space Shuttle and Space Ship Company was a space factory built up just for alien transportation and to help out Earth as well. The Enterprise was considered very prominent in space, very lucrative and a space gold mine. For this reason, it had the resources to help Earth build their own space shuttles. While Earth's space factory was in South San Jose, California, the space Enterprise was located on Jupiter and the planet made space shuttle parts for California's factory on Earth. But the alien monarch that owned the spacecraft Enterprise saw a problem rising in Earth's future of the 1980s. The aliens on this planet were clairvoyant beings and they could see a major malfunction happening with one of Earth's space shuttles. And they could see this actually centuries before the fact. So the Jupiter monarchy planned to build an adjacent part of their own spacecraft Enterprise just for Earth's 1986 space shuttle that they predicted would dissipate in flame in mid-air because of a faulty ring in one of the auxiliary engines. The adjacent part of the spacecraft factory had a building or a room that produced the perfect ring for Earth's space shuttle, and they just kept producing round rubber rings in the hopes of producing the perfect ring for Earth's space shuttle, the Challenger. They also made auxiliary engines and they just kept producing them over and over until they had the perfect take-apart engines for the Challenger. They did this work repeatedly because of safety measures and to redo one's work was like finding the perfect space piece to a space shuttle that would work and not malfunction. The Alien Queen had been placed on her Jupiter throne by receiving the monarchy from her parents and she had also inherited Earth's Challenger mission from her father, which his family had started centuries ago. And because of this space was a sensitive benefactor if it felt it needed to save Earth's Challenger from a clairvoyant futuristic calling from centuries ago. The other reason why the aliens of centuries ago wanted to help Earth's space shuttle of 1986 was because of the circumstances of the only African American astronaut to board it. Jupiter had taken a profound liking to Earth's Africa because it was the first continent on the planet and the most powerful. Jupiter also wanted to help the African people because of the way Earth had displaced them. So Jupiter stepped up the game of wanting to assist the life circumstances that were surrounding the only black astronaut aboard the Challenger because the continent of Africa needed to be healed in space's eyes.

And Jupiter played a role when it came to Earth's Africa. Since

Jupiter shone like a bright light in the Universal skies, it was because it was a light guiding the way because it has been around for over centuries. This fact could help Africa on Earth and the people that live there and are from there. Planet Jupiter is the one responsible for the overseeing of Earth's space shuttle, the Challenger, and the only African American onboard it. Jupiter had been planning for this day, that the space shuttle takes off, since the beginning of time. That's because each planet in space has a mission, most particularly, Earth. Since planet Earth had so much wrong with it in terms of wars, famine, violence and other injustices, it was the job of other planets to help Earth when those injustices arose. And, as for Jupiter, its focus was Earth's space shuttle that would launch in 1986 and predictably malfunction in mid-air. Earth's space shuttle was also of importance to Jupiter because it involved Africa. So Jupiter's mission was to assist both the space shuttle and the black astronaut and his family. And before the astronaut was even born, Jupiter of course knew of him and his black mother. Together with the forces of Saturn, the planets thought up a strategy that would bring about positive fates for both the Challenger and the African brother on board. And from the ground up, and brick by brick, Jupiter built a spacecraft factory which was funded by the Jupiter Monarch and owned by them as well. They built the spacecraft factory in the name of preserving their mission on Earth which was the Challenger and the black astronaut onboard it. It was like life revolved around Earth's spacecraft and the African American onboard it. Jupiter also communicated with the compass of both the sun and the moon for both to hit their rays on the spacecraft factory for support and life giving force. And the parents of the future queen of Jupiter oversaw everything of the factory's making so that they could pass on their mission factory to their daughter, Aluna

28

Grace. Jupiter held steadfast in its own Monarch and the Monarchy saw to it that it stayed Jupiter's government for many centuries into the future for the sake of Earth's Challenger and the black brother onboard. For this, Jupiter and the rest of space did not back down until missions were accomplished, the planets were perfectly in line with what to do in times of Earth's crisis, and carried out their vision and clairvoyant prophecies until all was done and laid down future foundations. Jupiter was really strong like this, like a solidarity fist being thrown in the air for power and justice. And to speak of power, Jupiter looked deep from within and found its power there, where it also found its power in wanting to see justice for Earth's Challenger, for Africa, and there was so much power in being kind and giving and Jupiter knew it.

Africa was very attractive to Jupiter because its land was rolling and it had lucrative minerals like diamonds, phosphate rocks, platinum-group metals, bauxite and cobalt. Africa also produces other affluent minerals such as iron ore, gold and copper. Also Africa is rich in the history of the human race, and the aliens on Jupiter had a keen interest in the first humans on planet Earth. Beside the early humans' ghosts echoing in Jupiter's present, Jupiter also liked the fact that there were many beautiful animals on the continent of Africa like the zebra pounding their hooves toward the evening sunset, lions and hyenas. Jupiter couldn't understand why this continent was so rich in resources but at the same time treated so badly by others on Earth. Jupiter also had an understanding of pain, pain of persecution if found out, pain of the galaxy's past and pain of alien history. Jupiter saw Africa as a mirror image of struggle and of valiant vision because of that struggle. Because of this Jupiter wanted to incorporate Africa in its mission of helping not only the country but the men who represented it like the only African American aboard the Challenger. Jupiter saw both the country of Africa and the fateful space shuttle as a huge project to keep in mind, for not only safety reasons but social justice as well. Jupiter was also intrigued by the aspects of beauty in Africa, where the African women beautified themselves very differently to the Western woman. Jupiter also took a liking to the simple dress code of Africa and how African mothers balanced water jugs on their heads, while their breasts showed like half-moons. Jupiter was also in love with the fact that the sun directly faced the land of Africa, making the African people dark and so close resembling the power of the sun and what it can do. Jupiter saw the weaving, the sowing and the magic of the sun and how it lifted up the people of Africa in its image and gave them power. Jupiter could feel this power and Jupiter claimed this power as their own as they set out to help Earth's Africa in need of celestial support. In the eyes of the alien gods, Jupiter and Africa were never too far apart from each other as the sunsets and sunrises of Africa hit the surface of Jupiter and the light would bounce back and forth on Jupiter and the great body of Africa. And underneath the magnetic field of Africa, signals would communicate with Jupiter's satellites and the two made a plan for both the space shuttle and the black family with roots from Africa. And like the dusty, tannish brown rolling land of Africa and its many resources such as the gold and the diamonds, Jupiter wanted to see to it justice served like the justice preserved in the gold and the diamonds. For Africa, even though politically disenfranchised, was Earth's leader and Jupiter wanted to make sure Africa's power was firmly implemented back in place for the sake of truth, for the sake of peace.

Jupiter also had a keen interest in Africa, because Jupiter also had a deep interest in helping Africa in times of violence, hunger and the curtailing of economic growth in the country. Jupiter knew of the wars in Sudan, South Sudan, Somalia, the Congo and the Central African Republic. All of this, including the corruption and bribery among African officials, is what galvanized Jupiter to its feet when it came to Africa. Jupiter also wanted to know why the rest of the planet Earth would not help Africa, the way space wanted to help Africa. Among the leading developed Nations of Earth, Africa was still the most underdeveloped and the least powerful, even though it was the first inhabited continent of planet Earth. With this fact, Jupiter thought that surely Africa should be the most powerful and not the most disenfranchised. Jupiter would roar with rolling storms in its skies with the way it felt about how Africa was being treated on Earth. Jupiter's heart would pulse within its core when thinking just of Africa. And for centuries the planet was preparing just for Africa, since that's how most of space operates: by planning on assisting planet Earth in times of need and based on space prophecies. Although the rest of space was not completely innocent of wars, it did know how to bounce back from violence and in Jupiter's case the planet sat still and peaceful for centuries as it prepared to help Earth with Africa and its space shuttle in the 1980s. As Jupiter enjoyed its many years of peace, it also lamented alongside Earth of the wars in Africa, the infliction of violence onto its own people, and the malfunction of a future space shuttle. Also the conflicts in Africa would shake Jupiter to its core, and then the entire planet would cry as the stars seemingly fell out of space and straight down as rain and breaking Earth's surface. The tears that were made of the gassy stars in space were so heavy at the thought of Africa that the stars themselves shunned Earth for the treatment of the African people. Because Jupiter knew that Africa was a great continent because it was the first and for this Jupiter saw Africa as a leader and not an underdog. The monarchy on Jupiter wanted to see that African ghosts were raised up in the name of justice and affluency, peace and the diminishing of war, violence and political conflict. And of course there was the Jupiter Monarch's project of assisting the space shuttle from its launch pad and straight into its neighbors in space. Jupiter knew it could not play around and be idle when it came to its African and Challenger mission; Jupiter had Earthly wounds to mend before it could take a break in space. It was like distance time traveling for Jupiter when it came to helping Africa, it was not to be stopped until a mission accomplished.

Actually, Earth can see Jupiter and the moon in the night skies since Jupiter is the one planet that has such an interest in helping Earth. The moon could work with Jupiter, in a way that would assist planet Earth. Together, the moon and Jupiter could work their magic when it came to helping Earth's Africa and the fateful space shuttle in the 1980s. Jupiter is about 240,000 miles away from the moon and it would take about six hundred days to actually get to Jupiter from where Earth is at. The moon is closest to Earth by a mere 233000 miles away while Jupiter is 373 million away from planet Earth. There are believed to be seventy-nine moons total to Jupiter but Jupiter knows it must keep working with the main moon and together with that moon curtail all hardship coming Earth's way in the forms of wars, violence and a host of other injustices. If Earthlings can see both the moon and Jupiter at night, that is a sure sign of progress toward peace and the diminishing of future conflict. Jupiter knows its agenda by heart, and it is only in space can Jupiter spin its work for the sake of planet Earth. Even though Jupiter is so many miles away from the moon it can shine bright like a star in Earth's nightly skies alongside the moon. While Jupiter likes to work with the main moon on helping planet Earth, Jupiter's own moons orbit around the planet while Jupiter works its magic in helping both Africa and the space shuttle. Jupiter has its own moons with interesting names like Metis, Adrastea, Amalthea and Thebe. As Jupiter plans ahead to save Africa and the infamous 1986 Earthly space shuttle, its own moons takes several hours to orbit around Jupiter. Jupiter's moons are lovely in colors like purple, multi-colored, red and yellow. Together, all of Jupiter's moons create a colorful palate that undulates onto Jupiter itself and enhances the planet's beauty and most importantly its wit. While Jupiter recognizes the beauty of its own seventy-nine moons, it also will never stop working with the main moon to bring Earth what it needs and restore Africa's power on Earth. As the many colored Jupiter moons make their orbit around Jupiter they never cease in the help of planet Earth by the very heart of Jupiter. Jupiter's own moons serve as a conduit of hope and hard work of the bestowing of Jupiter onto Earth's Africa. Jupiter's moons never stop their hours long orbit because they know it will keep the 1986 space shuttle intact, and keep Africa the most powerful continent on planet Earth. The moons know they never give up orbiting around Jupiter, if they want to see justice done for Earth. And as for the main moon, in space, in Earth's sky both night and day, it will continue to work hard in the name of Jupiter's will for Earth, for Africa and for the Challenger.

And as for Aluna Grace, her parents put her in charge of Jupiter's moons, to see to it that the moons orbit around the planet in a timely fashion. For the alien brain is complicated like that, and brilliant. The alien brain can help its own planet's moons circulate and orbit around the way they are supposed to. For Jupiter's seventy-nine moons were essential in helping not only Jupiter but planet Earth as well. And Aluna Grace saw to it that each moon played a role in the undulation of power toward Jupiter's surface for the causes of peace and the diminishing of conflict and all in the name of assisting planet Earth. The yellow surface of Jupiter's moon Lo was like the power of the sun onto the planet and it gave it life force and meaning. And the pinkish red color of the moon Amalthea gave it fury and fire but everything nice that goes into furies for the sake of giving fuel and energy to planet Earth's causes. And as for the orange red solidness of the Cyllene, it also gave fuel to the fire when the plans for planet Earth were made by Aluna Grace and her seventy-nine moon entourage. And the moon Philophrosyne seemed to be on constant fire to keep wars and other injustices at bay for planet Jupiter in the hopes that Jupiter will remain a utopia so it can help Earth. Aluna Grace never faltered in her step when circulating Jupiter's moons around and she was consistent with their orbits and timed each one for the hours it took to get around the planet. She knew that keeping the moons in check and balance would keep Jupiter afloat, but most importantly the moons' orbits would serve as a merry go round in consistency for the sake of Earth's own will. In all actuality it was Jupiter's will that wanted the best outcomes for Earth, whether political or social Jupiter would see to it that Earth will have its day of justice and justice will be served through the seventy-nine moons' orbits as they pass through Jupiter's realm. Aluna Grace was in charge of this rodeo of the orbiting of the seventy-nine moons, and she used her alien brain that was figuratively bigger than the gods so that she could win the many past wars of planet Earth. And the yellow of Lo, and the pink and red of Amalthea and the fires of Philophrosyne all contributed to Aluna Grace's cause for Earth and she saw to it to the ends of the Universe. And each of the seventy-nine moons to the last of the moons all made their orbit around Jupiter in the hopes of finding answers to planet Earth's wars and social ills and problems. Jupiter's seventy-nine moons never stopped rotating around and around until they cooked up a big plate of justice for Earth, so that the rest of the Universe would remain in peace for centuries going forward.

Aluna Grace gives way for one of Jupiter's moons, Europa, to give reflection to Jupiter's surface. Europa's icy surface gives reflection to itself and Jupiter. The moon is millions of years old which makes it relatively young compared to the trillions and trillions of years space has been around. Aluna Grace never gives up on any of her moons, for she knows that their grace and their style help not only Jupiter but Earth as well. She ponders on the fact that Europa is a young moon compared to her family's monarch in place in space for so many eons of centuries that she appreciates the perspective of a young and upcoming moon that also orbits around Jupiter. The ice that coats Europa's surface cools off any heated disarray of the elements that would hinder Jupiter. And Jupiter knows that Europa is relative in helping the planet turn around in its orbit. And Aluna Grace knows the fact that the ice that inhabits the Europa moon can act as an armor or a shield in its own defense. She also knows that the icy surface can break away from the moon and cause icicles to rain throughout Jupiter's realm. When this happens she knows it can cause friction but at the same time cool off the fires from the other moon that gives off fire. Aluna Grace works with the icy condition of Europa for the sake of having ice as a blessing in Jupiter's atmosphere. The ice could coagulate up into Jupiter's aura and make it rain ice crystals. It would be like raining ice storms on the planet and giving Jupiter a dark side. Aluna Grace could turn the ice into snow, rain or even harden the icicles into a diamond-like fashion and other faux jewels. All of this would contribute to Jupiter's character and landscape. And as for Europa, the young moon, she would be blessing Jupiter's orbit and enriching Jupiter's circumstances. Europa is a tan color with white clouds on it, and she would pulse out the tan and white colors like a light brown flashlight in between the space of Jupiter and the young moon. And the distance between Europa and the moon could mean that distance would take the same amount of time to show in Earth's skies. And there is still Africa that Europa could influence with its innocent ice and young age. As Europa turns around Jupiter, every step it takes toward completion of the orbit will only assist Africa in the end, for Europa's young age can splash space purity onto Africa like a tulip in a dawn.

Aluna Grace also overlooks Jupiter's other moon, Callisto. Callisto could hold humanity because it is forty percent water and may have an underground ocean. Made of water, ice and rocks the moon is one of Jupiter's largest. It also shines brighter than Earth's moon because of its ice reflecting the sun. Aluna Grace realizes that Callisto is such an asset to Jupiter's cause of assisting planet Earth because Earthlings could actually live there. So she takes Callisto's reflections from the sun and dangles the reflections like lanky long crystals in front of Earth in order to out stretch Callisto's reflection to Earth in mayday times. Callisto is Aluna Grace's favorite moon because it is so close to humanity because of its large body of water. Aluna Grace rides the water off of Callisto to billow out strength to Earth and to awaken peace. She knows that the water on Callisto is such an important element when it comes to helping Earth. For water has secrets folded in its waves and can be dark blue, gray and green and give off a watery spell for Earth and Aluna Grace knows it. Callisto's surface is so old but so wise at the same time. Because of this the moon rises up in Jupiter's realm as a big moon full of pride and of course Aluna Grace's joy. It is also known as the "dead moon" and the underground ocean theory gives it mystery and depth. Beneath Callisto's surface may the mysterious ocean work its magic in being in a casket-like ground where only vampires of the sort roam and give their secrets a crushing blow to Callisto's surface for the truth to crack outwardly. And when this happens may the Universe open up to the open grave of Callisto's underground and spread about the art of death in a way that helps understand the humans dying and being buried in the ground much like Callisto's core and underground ocean. Because of Callisto's underground magic, it gives the rest of space meaning when it comes to death and dying. Because even in space the life cycle must move on, all things die and are born. And Aluna Grace knows that when her parents naturally leave their thrones, she will take over the Space Shuttle and Space Ship Company for the sake of Earth's Africa and the Challenger. And with her large alien brain she can either curtail the underground waters of Callisto or bring them forward for the health that water brings not just for space but for Earth as well. For she also knows that the dead moon is not dead, but indeed alive because of the water it embodies and holds both on its surface and underneath. For this, Aluna Grace makes friends with Callisto because she knows she needs the element and the magic of water when it comes time to help planet Earth. Earth has water on its surface, as well, and it makes a match for Callisto's water both on the surface and in its core. May the water of both Earth and Callisto steam up into both their atmospheres and be sword of peace in front of storms.

Of course Aluna Grace has her hands full when it comes to Jupiter's other moon, Valetudo. By the pull of the planet Jupiter, Valetudo is able to show its face to the solar system. It takes twelve million miles for Valetudo to make an orbit and it also takes about one and a half years for it to make a full orbit around Jupiter. But the reason why Aluna Grace has her hands full is because Valetudo is a retrograde moon, meaning that it can collide with other retrograde moons while in orbit. It also orbits backwards which could cause Aluna Grace confusion. But together with the pull of the planet and the collision with other moons, Aluna Grace can come up with creative ways to distribute all the moon's collisions to benefit planet Earth. And like most of Jupiter's moons, Valetudo is made of ice, water, and rocks. The water is a sure sign that Aluna Grace would have magic to work with when helping Earth, and the ice would be like those former long lanky crystals she could tangle like crystals and the light of the crystals would billow out into space and hit Earth's surface. While the moon Valetudo is almost like an oddball moon, because of its backwards orbit, it also can serve as a valiant vision for Earth, since Earth as well is backwards with all its wars, violence and inhumanities. Valetudo's backwards movement can create positive energy for the solar system and then the system will work well with planet Earth. And as Valetudo crisscrosses with other moons during its own orbit, this effect could create even more magic for Jupiter and for Earth as well. For all the moons that collide together in the name of the orbit can create energy like a magnetic force curtailing Earth's atrocities and giving power back to Africa. For the moon's pull can gravitate on Earth and keep Earthlings grounded whole hearted. Because the several moons that touch base with each other during a collision especially if they all have water on them, the wateriness can hit Earth's moon and then Earth's moon's light would hit the planet's water and cast out peace and justice. And as for Aluna Grace and Valetudo they both work together to find the perfect glove to fit the hand of planet Earth when it comes time to hold that chalice in the horizon of utopian peace. And the twelve million miles that Valetudo makes to get around Jupiter is a signal that all is well with Jupiter's realm and the millions of miles it takes and after its finish is like giving the greenlight to continue working with planet Earth.

Aluna Grace also had smaller moons to work with when it came to oversee the orbiting of all of Jupiter's moons. Adrastea is one of Jupiter's smaller inner moons of the planet's four inner moons. It takes less than a day to orbit around Jupiter and only one side of Adrastea is facing Jupiter as it orbits around. This moon also orbits around at the edge of Jupiter's main ring. Adrastea is also irregular in shape, making it like a natural pearl effect because natural pearls are irregular in shape as well. Aluna Grace sees this moon like a mother of pearls because when looking through the Galileo spacecraft it doesn't say much of what it's made of, but shows like a misshapen pearl. With the speed and the time it takes Adrastea to make the orbit around Jupiter, Aluna Grace is on top of her game. This is because Adrastea makes the orbit around in record time, and like the speed of light the moon ceases to fail in its quest to get around Jupiter in less than a day. Aluna Grace knows that the fast timing of this particular moon can pose a challenge when sending outer space waves of delight to planet Earth because the moon moves faster than the typical moon. With the other moons she can calculate in good time the strength of the moon's wavelengths in order to assist planet Earth because possibilities arise in their slowness. However, with Adrastea it is harder for Aluna Grace to know what this moon can do for Earth since she moves so fast. Adrastea was named after the foster mother of the Greek god, Zeus. Perhaps this is the reason why the moon is so fast and only takes a day to get around Jupiter. For Zeus was an omnipotent God, shaking the realms of space to its edges, and possibly even causing havoc for space as well. And for this moon to be named after Zeus's mother is like an epic Roman territorial issue with both space and the energy of Zeus's mythology. But Aluna Grace finds creative ways to work with history and the energy of Adrastea. She can take the moon's orbital path that it leaves behind, and turn it into the positive energy of planet Earth. She can follow its light like she can its orbit and look into its one-sided face as it orbits her planet and wish the moon and herself well, like a prayer given out into the rest of space. And she always sees its face because it does not turn while in orbit, and she can always look into Adrastea's continents and speak the alien language of good will and good faith, especially when it comes to helping out planet Earth. Aluna Grace can also work with the Galileo spacecraft to better understand Adrastea for the sake of using the full benefits of this particular moon. Aluna Grace also sees the moon like a piece of pearl from a string of pimpled-shaped balls that are not shaped perfectly like Adrastea and this is beauty to her.

Aluna Grace definitely has a very big moon in Jupiter's realm called Ganymede. This moon is considered the largest moon in the solar system and the ninth largest object in space as a whole. This moon is so large it doesn't even have an atmosphere. And it has more water than all of Earth's oceans, but to no avail because the water on Ganymede is mostly frozen. The moon has a metallic iron core with a rock shell and ice on top. Although Aluna Grace can work with the frozen water to better plan for the justice of Earth. For water elements, including when frozen, can carry the weight of the essences of life forward into meaning. The largest moon in space just happens to be Aluna Grace's project in moving forward projects for Earth and for humankind. The moon's vastness and outstretched figurative arms can hold Earth like clutching the peace that is there and for centuries, because Ganymede is so big. And in the largeness of this moon it takes not just the space around Jupiter, but most of Aluna Grace's time. And like the way Aluna Grace is the Alien Queen, this moon seems to match her wit with its bigness and brightness. Ganymede is actually Aluna Grace's favorite moon because, and to repeat, it matches her greatness as queen. And being an Alien Queen of Jupiter is like being queen of all space. Shall all life forms on other planets kiss the ground that Aluna Grace walks on or flies on. Aluna Grace could stand on top of Ganymede and reign her power positively and for the sake and the justices of Earth. Ganymede is large enough to carry Aluna Grace's queen status and weight. Both Aluna Grace and Ganymede are a match for each other and the atmosphere of Jupiter could diminish because of this moon's largeness, but it does not. This is because, as Aluna Grace walks the golden alien carpet, the atmosphere of Ganymede can finally open up and make way for the alien utopian peace queen. And it is all in the name of peace, peace for Jupiter and for Earth and may the largest moon in the solar system billow out its moonly waves onto the peace cause. And as for the frozen over water of Ganymede, it only is a welcoming sign of the hope of life for Earth to want to turn to. And the frozen tips of water waves poke straight up into Jupiter's atmosphere as a white flag for the end of chaos, wars, and the indication of the assistance of Earth. The moon Ganymede is like a big space god that speaks in large syllables for the sake of getting a point across. This moon never fails in its large space godly language for the big round sphere that is called Ganymede can hold up to trillions of years of space knowledge like a huge sea sponge soaks up water like a brain.

And there are Jupiter moons that have accidently come across Jupiter's orbit, like a crash, and one of these moons is Cyllene. Cyllene is a Jupiter moon that is also from an asteroid that just happened to join in on all the moon's orbit of Jupiter. Cyllene is 14.8 million miles away from Jupiter and it takes 752 Earth days to make one complete orbit. Aluna Grace knows that the slower pace of Cyllene can make the moon's waves undulate out into the rest of space, giving it good grace and just like most of the other moons. For being a moon, especially at a slower pace, can make time for positive energy to curl up and round space and Earth like the way moonlight hits water surfaces. Even though Cyllene is millions of miles away from Jupiter, it works well with Jupiter because of all the time it has to make the orbit around the planet. And all of the time it takes to spin around Jupiter could spin tales of its journey and the energy it leaves in its path as a testimony to Earth. Aluna Grace knows that the 752 Earth days buys her time to raise up good deeds and aspirations for planet Earth. And with the path that Cyllene leaves behind, as she orbits, Aluna Grace can follow suit and take whatever memories lie in that Cyllene's peaceful-like wake or path. Cyllene, as with all the other moons, makes space vibrant and reluctant in the face of death that may encapsulate space. Because all the moons, including Cyllene, show proof of life onboard the life ports of space, and they never cease to show otherwise. This is because all the moons alongside Cyllene are alive and well, showing their faces to the big realm of Jupiter. The lights and the colors of all the moons' surfaces show, in fact, vibrant life in space, and worthwhile life that could assist in the dangers of planet Earth. That is why Aluna Grace's family's Alien Monarchy works hard with the moons to bring about justice and peace for Earth with all the moons' orbits' help. For their lunar pull hits the waters of Earth and shift hardship at its core, and then shows the alien face in the moonlit sky, but only at a distance. Shall humanity reconcile with the colors in the skies above them as alien help as their moons take shape as if to finally show their faces?

Of course, Aluna Grace has plenty of moons that broke apart during a collision into Jupiter's realm, but they have become a group of moons under the same name per se. The Ananke moon is also a retrograde moon, in that it orbits backwards around the planet. And like other retrograde moons it is irregular in shape. This moon was formally an asteroid which was more than likely pulled in by Jupiter's gravity. A major space collision, and to repeat, broke it into fifteen other moons and now it is a group of moons under the name Ananke. For Aluna Grace this is also a confusing task, because all fifteen moons orbit backwards, leaving a confusing light in their paths. The main Ananke moon is the largest moon of the entire group, making a glow. And with the glow that is a part of Ananke, Queen Aluna Grace weaves her magic into something nice for planet Earth. And with this main moon of Ananke, Aluna Grace can ride its coattails of being a former asteroid from deep space. Because being a former asteroid that has traveled throughout space is like having prominence and wisdom. And Aluna Grace knows this and so she harnesses this

43

energy from the former space rock. And as far as the collision, Aluna Grace takes advantage of it because the moon is now in Jupiter's orbital realm. And Aluna Grace doesn't mind that Ananke is unusual in shape, because, and to repeat, natural pearls are irregular in shape and size as well. To her, she could wear all fifteen Ananke moons like a string of pearls and the reflection from the pearls, or the moon's surface, can hit Earth's Africa in a pearly graceful way. As all the Ananke moons make their retrograde orbits around Jupiter, may they leave behind a peaceful wake of wisdom, since they are wise from being from a former traveling asteroid anyway. Under the space management of Aluna Grace, she makes way for the retrograde moons' backwards orbits to better assist planet Earth, and the endearing endeavor which is Africa. The backwards orbit efforts are a collective group work that entails the gravity or the pull of Jupiter. May the Ananke moon group work well with Aluna Grace's good intentions when it comes to helping the dark side of Earth and mistreatment of Earth's Africa. And may the backwards orbits of the Ananke group send out waves of kindness and love toward the downtrodden Africa, but may those moon's waves undulate power back to Africa which once was rich in not just minerals, diamonds, and gold, but rich with the first signs of humanity. And the wisdom of the former asteroid, that has more than likely traveled space open wide, brings about the wisdom of doing injustices done to Africa like a disarming. And in the light of the Ananke's path may the largest moon in the group of all fifteen moons be the leader of sending the peace signal to Earth and above all to Africa (all facts on moons NASA or Wikipedia).

Chapter 1

It's the early 1900s and, somewhere in space, they are far more advanced. They already have solar panels on satellites with communication receptors built in them. These communication receptors inside the alien satellites bounce off of both Jupiter and Saturn as the two planets watch as events unfold within either planet and on Earth as well. Within the realms of Saturn and Jupiter the Alien fellowship is clairvoyant at best and can see Earth's future as their satellites report back to them. For something in the ground and the magnetic field within Earth has been transmitting communication back and forth with Saturn and Jupiter. And beneath Earth's surface there are constant shifts in the land that sends signals to Jupiter's satellites and thus the Alien fellowship can predict the future for Earth. Long before Earth realized the benefits of space, other beings in outer space have taken advantage of all space can sow and reap in the name of the alien solar panels that are built on alien satellites. At once Saturn knew nothing of life on Jupiter and vice versa but they discovered each other through alien technology that was being used in space long before Earth did. So the alien life on Saturn and Jupiter welcomed each other and shared technology secrets, and most importantly space technology secrets. The Saturn Alien King and the Jupiter Alien Queen made sure there was like an alien utopia happening between the two planets with equality reigning supreme among the Space Alien fellowships. The Alien King and the Alien Queen agreed that equality among all alien life forms between the two planets was the only way to prevent frictions like war and violence. One could say that the king and queen from both planets made a peace pact in order to keep both planets going and living a long time almost like eternity and with no end in sight. Jupiter was the first to come up with the solar panel satellites in space and then shared their discovery with Saturn. They both realized that the satellites were picking up on Earth's activities and the king and queen realized they could tell Earth's future based on being clairvoyant beings but also by the patterns that Earth was repeating. Not only were the satellites giving information about their own planets but they were also picking up on the rifts and shifts of Earth's magnetic field and so the Alien fellowship was watching with a keen and hopeful eye. The Jupiter Alien Queen was sort of like Earth's Cleopatra in that she made peace settlements and did political business with Saturn's Alien King. The Jupiter Queen was also very unhappy to see the unnerving events against females on Earth, since she had come from a place of peace. While Cleopatra came to Marc Anthony by rolling herself up in a carpet the Jupiter Queen presented herself to the Saturn King by air waves in space and communicating with him via the satellite that was positioned between the two planets whereas she then presented to him the first kind of femaleness that space has ever known. Together the king and queen forged a romantic relationship based in space and made an avowal to justice for Earth and based on the patterns of Earth they knew their plates were full.

The Alien King and Queen from both Saturn and Jupiter had a love so strong that it played a role once both the king and queen decided to take on the task which was Earth. And with their satellites they picked up on Earth's first World War and America's first president being shot which all happened in the

46

early 1900s in which the aliens were showing leadership throughout space with their satellite technology. Following World War I, the aliens watched Earth repeat its pattern of war with World War II in the early 1920s. Then came the Korean War and the ever so unpopular war which would be Vietnam to follow suit. Earth's patterns were really registering with the Alien fellowship and the aliens knew they had to do something about hindering events they thought they could control. Besides satellite technology the aliens had a way with intercepting the dreams of humans and communicating with them privately through nature. The aliens could also possess animals and humans on Earth but only under necessary circumstances. For the aliens had been around since prehistoric times and this is how they could transform themselves to be among humanity in a secretive way and their communication skills were learned through traveling centuries and centuries of space and time. The Alien King and Queen that had bestowed an equal alien society on their planets were devastated as they had to watch the wars on Earth and presidents being assassinated. Earth, to them, seemed like a baby planet and a planet that needed help and that was bursting at the seams if not helped. So the king and queen started to strategize a plan to help the falling-apart Earth. Unknown to Earth they created invisible satellites that circulated around Earth, because their satellites were limited as to the whole picture of what was happening on Earth. And they secretly used solar panels on these satellites to help Earth with energy from both space and the sun. With the invisible satellites up and working around Earth's sphere, the Alien King and Queen could watch events as they unfolded but they could also watch Earth's patterns so that they could accurately predict future events. Although Earth's patterns were not needed for the Alien King and Queen completely because they were already clairvoyant beings that could see into the future. For an example they knew that Hitler would be stealing art during World War II and where he would be storing that stolen work. They also knew that Hitler stealing artwork would be like the blueprint of many artists, in the future, being stolen from. They could see into the 1980s of whites stealing artistic ideas from black artists and all the way into the millennium. So the king and queen decided that they needed to put together a task force of aliens that investigate creative thefts and to try to hinder the thefts as well. The king and queen also knew they had to put a specialized task force of alien investigators to use their clairvoyant gifts to watch out for major catastrophes on Earth that they can hinder by privately communicating with humans.

Chapter 2

The alien investigation of artistic theft on Earth was to be taken seriously by the Alien King and Queen because they knew it would curtail the greed of white power and return power to the black communities, most particularly in America since all the thefts seem to be taking place there and after Hitler had laid down a blueprint for it by way of conduit of war and influence onto America. So the king and queen put together their own alien artistic theft task force right at the start of the Great Migration and the Harlem Renaissance. They knew that the Great Migration would return power back to African Americans after they fled the South, and to firmly implement that freedom the king and queen saw that the Harlem Renaissance that would follow the Migration needed by all means to be protected. The African Renaissance would consist of poets, prose writers, singers, models and musicians. The king and queen predicted that the Renaissance would take shape after the American Civil War and they saw clearly that it could be taken from the blacks by means of returning the power of evil of slavery. So the alien artistic task force would put alien agents on Earth in the form of nature, humanity and the animal kingdom to assist the blacks as they embarked on their newfound journey of freedom after bondage and slavery. The king and queen called upon their most sensitive and intelligent and aesthetic minded alien kin to join their artistic task force. The task force would consist of some several hundred aliens to transform themselves on Earth as they were to help black Americans in their creative endeavors in the Harlem Renaissance. They were ordered by the king and queen to take the form of domestic animals that live with black artists and to take form as leaves on trees to glitter in the sun and serve as alien assistance and like solar panels for the black artists. They were to possess flowers and plants that sat around the black artists' homes to waver out creative inspiration. Other aliens were to be like detectives when art was stolen from black artists of the Harlem Renaissance and they were to bring justice and shed light on the thefts via helping African Americans standing up for themselves. Other aliens would embody the brick of lavish Harlem buildings that black artists sang in so that their voices would bounce off the brick walls like a message from the Universe. And wherever the aliens could take shape or form to help the black artists they were to use the form creatively to either stop thefts from happening or to give voice to the black artists if their work was stolen. The task force was carefully tailored to fit the needs of African Americans after dealing with the Civil War. And the king and queen wanted to distill their space utopia onto Harlem so that the blacks could remain free from political violence, war and slavery.

The Alien Queen could see into the future: Natasha Brown, a mixed woman with both black and white within her. Natasha Brown was born in Morningside Heights of Harlem where it is an enriched black neighborhood of New York City. It was also the early 1920s when Natasha was born and right when the aliens had put up their space technology throughout their planets. Natasha's mother like so many other blacks was impacted by a Lunacy Institutionalization which was a common practice of putting blacks in mental hospitals after the Civil War. Her father was Irish American and had left her when she was a baby but had left her with her black grandmother in Harlem. Natasha favored her father's complexion and was passing for white even in Harlem. Although everyone in Harlem knew she was half black because they knew her mother and her grandmother. Her grandfather was away serving in World War II for the United States Army and during this time he did not play the role of a father for Natasha because he was away fighting Nazi Germany. He led the art investigations of World War II which entailed seizing back stolen artwork by the Nazis and returning them back to their owners and countries. This fact would be a pivotal moment in Natasha's childhood even though the grandfather wasn't around to help raise her. For it was the early 1940s and right after the Harlem Renaissance that celebrated African American art, music and poetry. And right before the Harlem Renaissance, Natasha's grandmother raised Natasha to be aesthetic in the arts and in poetry and prose. The grandmother knew about her husband leading the art investigations against the Germans, and she thought that in his absence she could at least bestow onto Natasha the importance of being creative and guarding one's work like the army soldiers were doing during the war. She taught her dance and finger painting the alphabet so that she could instill in her the poetic license. The little family also had a black and white Persian cat with a beautiful and full coat of hair that the queen sent to guard Natasha and her grandmother like a soldier standing outside an Embassy with a long gun. Yes, because aliens could embody the Persian cat and be a witness to Natasha's authenticity and to guard her life because something was amiss on her horizon. And the Alien Queen knew this because she could tell the future of Natasha's life so she sent the Persian cat as a guardian angel to protect not only Natasha's life but her creativity as well since it was so important toward the African American community of Harlem. Most particularly for the 1940s that were coming up in Natasha's near future as a dancer and writer in which she would contribute to the black arts

51

of Harlem. The queen knew that Natasha as an artist for the after lingerings of the Harlem Renaissance would pose a threat to white women as it was commonplace for white women to steal creative ideas from black women especially after the Great Migration happened in America and subsequently empowering blacks with their own artistic Renaissance.

The black Persian cat was there and everywhere in Natasha's childhood while she grew up in Harlem in the early 1920s. As Natasha grew from a girl and into a woman in the mid-to-late 1940s the cat was still around and would ride on Natasha's shoulders all throughout Harlem. When Natasha took dance classes, the cat was there. When Natasha wrote poetry and prose, the cat was still always there by her side and watching and waiting on the creative theft would soon consume Natasha's self-esteem and life. She would stroll along the Hudson River with the cat on her shoulders and watch as the birds skidded and landed on the surface of the river. Natasha took such good care of the Persian cat, she fed it by the river as she ate her own lunch. As Natasha attended the Dance Theatre of Harlem, the black cat was waiting in the wings of the dance floor and watching Natasha's every dance step. For the queen sent the Persian cat as a guardian and witness to what was about to happen to Natasha's creative abilities and endeavors. Natasha also studied creative writing at the College of New Rochelle near Harlem and between learning to dance and getting a writing degree, the cat was always there perched in a doorway or on Natasha's shoulders. The poems Natasha wrote in college were in a different format than most poetry sonnets. She interweaved poetry in prose form and wrote about controversial topics like black bodies hanging from Southern trees and how she herself feels that pain while she dances in sheer see-through olive-colored silk dresses since she had a light skin complexion for a black woman. She read aloud her poetry to the cat and the cat just perched on her bed with a whimsical demeanor because the cat already knew everything. As Natasha walked the New York City streets with the cat on her shoulder, this would give the cat a vantage view of any foreseen enemies in Natasha's path and yes even as she walked the city streets. The clear yellow liquid rays of sun funneled around Natasha and the light from the day moon hugged her limbs as well. It was the solar panels and the communication receptors on the alien's satellites that guided Natasha as she simply walked down the streets and the solar panels picked out the sun rays and would flourish around Natasha and the cat sitting on her shoulder. Even though the cat was looking out for thieves and danger, the cat also knew that the alien satellites equipped with solar energy from the sun would be like a shield to carry home. Both the cat and Natasha were inseparable from her childhood and into her early twenties as to when the Harlem Renaissance was in its after lingerings. As Natasha veered past dance school and into public performance, whether on Harlem stages or in Harlem's streets, the cat served as a conduit of protection from the alien moon and the Universe.

Natasha wrote a poem about her Persian cat and how she felt it was a premonition of her future. Black nights, black skies reflect my Persian cat as the stars are tucked away in the blackness and all you can see is my cat remaining still at my side, she wrote. My cat's eyes are pools of blackness that look like crystal balls at the same time and as I look into his eyes it is like a kaleidoscope. My Persian is always at my side even in my weeping moments and even when I dance my arms branch out like long winding arms of trees that continue to weep. And the pain of my people at the Southern Oak is what my Persian can feel and see, and his very being gives me hope. My Persian is black like my race and as black as space and he is like a vehicle to the moon because his color reflects the moon's atmosphere. My cat perches on his hind legs and is still in a penurious moment

53

of my life as he sits there and watches everything. My dear black Persian would dissipate the sun into specks for me. Because it caused me too much pain as I sweltered and sweltered under it whether I was dancing on still like an artificial peace. My black Persian knows the pulsing veins of my heart and its redness spills its blood out like the energy of a graying river. My cat has warned me of skies turning from blue to black and purple like a bruise in the sky of a distant horizon and future. My Persian knows when my smile is faked or forced because my cat can feel my soul crying at passing for white while a black woman during post Harlem Renaissance. And when I dance my Persian is at my side watching and contemplating every dance step. It's as if my dancing feet send echoes up into space where the black skies look down on me because it wants to pull me up while gravity keeps me grounded like an injustice. May the pink sky after any given storm open up and show its own heart bleeding red and show my pain. And my dear black Persian knows my pain so well if it were his own and we weep together. Curled up on my shoulders my black cat feels what it is like to ride a human and to be human on such bare shoulders. My black cat is a symbol like a large cat in the wilderness that climbs alongside mountain goats on the sides of huge mountain facades. This is because my cat's soul has faced as much adversity as mine did, and my cat knows how to persevere like the way I do through my artistic abilities. In the end my black cat is my tunnel of strength from within where inside those winding twisting veins lead to my pulsing bloody heart.

Chapter 3

Natasha wrote poems, since she wanted to be a part of the aftermath of the Harlem Renaissance and so she wrote poetry about being black but passing for white. My father's color is like a big masking green plant that covers my true color and the plant's palm is like the sun covering the moon and all you see is lightness. My father's heritage weighs me down as I try to show the world my Africana side, like a herd of African zebras trotting toward the dawn. Their black and whiteness blends well together as the African evening clouds dissipate the sun and all is black again. I awake each morning with the hardship stuck in my throat, as I cannot explain why I am passing for white when I am supposed to look and be black. As the mornings arise, specks of yellow dots cover my white curtains and I can see the funnel of light from the sky speaking to me of my condition. The white curtains sit still on my window silent as my Caucasian side is quiet while the blackness inside me brews and brews and turns and burns within me. I cannot speak for the marginalized mulatto in me because it just is inside of me and can't be seen. And even though I look like this, I am one with the blood on the tree. For I have centuries of African blood flowing through me as the first great long journey out of Africa hit Europe and the sun was a distance away from that land and I became a victim of it. People say I don't look black but my hair is a half an afro and my face an Irish porcelain doll and the contrasts contradict each other and people say they are confused by me. Although I have seen my black grandfather twisted in his pain of black people's past and it has brought me to my knees even though people say I look white. And so I represent both the European world and the black world. And as my black grandmother raised me and walked me down the streets of the Morningside heights of Harlem other black folks knew the truth about me. And so they welcomed the poetry flying out my mouth on asphalt as a black hawk feminina flapping her wings like words found on African streets. And so they accepted me as their black next of kin the way you would identify a corpse at a morgue for crying out loud! As Harlem streets wept so did I even in my white and black condition and the former wars were never too far from me as I cried from my black soul even as my father's color covered me like an eclipse. And so my people in Harlem sang from their mouths like liquid butter and sophistication was beyond keeping at bay for black folk's talent could not be matched to none other. And the world bowed down and saluted the Great Migration which my grandparents were a part of and for only God's grace and sake.

It's not always easy to pass for white when all you want to do is to show the world you're black. When I've felt the world's anvil on my black spirit I know that I will return an Africana soul in the next life. And after shower storms the rainbow will peek through and shed light on my black side. There's much to do when you belong to black folks but pass for white it becomes like a reunion of the two. And black and white will surely find justice together even though lady justice is blind folded – she can't see what is really going on, all she can do is feel the injustice like that world anvil on my chest. Passing for white is like a life chore, in that I have to clean up after myself after my own personal storms have gone through and the lightning in the sky screeched through. Every day is a hassle as I pass for white because deep inside I know I am black and the echo inside of me whistles of the broken heartedness of my heart. As I dance on stage it is like my own personal revelation and Renaissance of myself. When the truncation of my black side took a fall and shattered into tiny pieces I rose up again, broken and playing like a backwards record. For the reasons why I pass for white belong to only God above and shall God see to my justice as I beg for my blackness back. I could stand still like a ghost at the side of the black panther and still I can only find my blackness from within. The Irish face is like a sheer pale slate of moon but only the paleness of the light that is seen at the moon's edges at night. My black and white Persian seems to be a reflection of me as his black and white coat humanizes him as I look into a mirror. The long black and white cat coat fits him like a tight fitted glove and I am the graceful hand. My black and white Persian and I pass for white together even though he is just a cat but he graces my life with a thick horizon and you can see my future in his eyes. Because of all this, my black and white Persian helps me through as I pass for white because his black and white fur is a spitting image of me and passes through the world smoothly. And to repeat, as my father's color has hid my black side for so long it is, in the end, the blackness that shows who I am. As California palms soak up the sun their greenness is a metaphor for me. This is because, as the sun shines on me as well, I darken easily and the California palm understands my black palm. As I raise my palm up to the sun in the sky I soak up its life giving rays much like the palm leaf that has a thick green coat on it.

When I dance on stage at the Cotton Club I know that I pass for white and nobody needs to tell me that because I should know. My eclipsed color as I dance gives off shadows of black people's past. And because I grew up in Harlem the black folks know my black soul and I am justified and restored. Dancing brings out the black sky in me as I dance on furious like a thunderstorm. I twirl and swirl my peach colored body on Harlem stages like a cyclone. And only black sensuality leaks out of my limbs as I dance the Harlem stage and then black men bleed at my heel that stands erect in the dancing shoe on stage. My half of afro sparkles underneath the lights that beat down like a funnel onto my very body as I dance the nights away like a snake curling to a beat. Even though I pass for white on the Harlem stage my black heart beats through and I wear it on my sleeve as I dance. I wear cultured pearls in my thick black curly hair and they fall like African teardrops as I dance and dance. There comes a time that while I am dancing and passing for white that my black heritage will stand out because justice is a long time coming. And as I dance, my black mother who is imprisoned in Lunacy Incarcerations dances out of me as well and I am projecting her pain of being locked up unjustly. Luckily for me my black grandparents raised me in the middle of Harlem so now I am allowed to dance the Harlem stages without being misunderstood in front of my people. As I dance, the Universe opens up above me and spills out black stars from its vessel and the black holes in space continue to spin deep for I am heavy in my dance step as my black spirit begs to be set free for I am still passing for white. Black ladies that watch me dance call me sister all the while I am still passing for white for they have known me and my black grandparents since I was a baby. Black ladies in the crowd wear jeweled crowns like Cleopatra and pearls fall from their foreheads as their eyeliner is drawn on like a cat. Harlem is not a black path to a gateway to some sort of Heaven but a turn key to the black soul that has been held in bondage for so long before the Renaissance and the Great Migration. And yes even though I pass for white I am second generation of the Great African Migration and it belongs to me as much as my black mother. As I dance I project the fact that I am black and from the black migration and I hold the Harlem Renaissance up in the air like a tight fist as a salute to not just the black cat but to God and the Universe. On stage the world is my puppet as I tell it what to do and say with the dance steps I make in the name of justice for African Americans that just escaped slavery.

If I could dance on top of the moon I would, its light shines and branches out onto Harlem stages. It inspires me and I know it fights for me because I talk to the gods that surround it when I look up at Harlem night skies. They say they know my soul so well since I am passing for white although deep down inside I am of the African American race. They tell me to keep dancing despite the adversity both inside and out of adversity. And when the blue and red lights shine on the dancing stage I know they are reflecting the same kind of light from the life-giving moon. The gods hold up the moon when blacks like me are passing for white and are feeling lost because of it. To dance on the moon is like being elevated up into space and coming back an enriched soulful dancer when once so close to the stars. When the moon shows its face either in blue days or black nights it shows Africa and black Americans its sympathy and understanding and it never ceases otherwise. As alien guards protect the moon and all its justice and glory, African Americans are singing and dancing down in Harlem. As the planets align together they circulate the moon even as I wish to dance on top of it with glee and talent. It's almost like the moon was made just for Harlem in the 1920s until some destructive force turned it around and then the moon faced another direction. The light of the smiling-faced moon touched the Hudson River at nights as black Americans sang and read poetry. The Gods are recognizable in African American poetry as they speak through black bodies. And so then the moon descends upward in space as the poetic words of blacks swing and turn and burn in the atmosphere that is Harlem. As I dance and speak my poetry there is the moon undulating with the waters on Earth and people can hear my black voice even though I am passing for white. There is not much I can do to change the fact that I am passing for white, although the moon sees right through to my black side and praises it like a moon dawn on space skies. Harlem in the 1920s is sitting beneath the moon as if it only belongs to Harlem for the day of justice has come through the Harlem Renaissance. And when I dance on New York City stages, my dancing feet echo straight up to the moon and that sound bounces back like a bang from space. For in space all is quiet until there is an injustice that interrupts it and then the moon becomes the manager of the fight for peace and justice. For there is so much to lose in the house of the moon and the gods know the liabilities that are plagued onto black Americans, yes even the ones that are passing for white.

Chapter 4

Natasha wore black and white clothing all around Harlem. She wore white suits with big thick black belts around her waist all the while her black Persian cat rode on her shoulders. She wore her black and white clothes with pride because she was both black and white. She made a black lace dress and wore it to special occasions like cocktail parties with black ladies from the black bourgeois. She knew how to sew and to design her own wardrobe just as well as she wrote poetry and danced. Sometimes she would walk down the streets of Harlem in one black heel and the other white while she wore a white satin dress with a black sash around her middle. She was the style queen of black and white fashion and people noticed her black and white wardrobe and they called her the street princess of black and white. She wore large-brimmed white hats with a black ribbon tied around the middle of the hat. She wore black and white dresses with diamond and checkered shapes on them. This was Natasha passing for white but showing her black side with the black patterns in her clothing. Some days she would even wear one black sock and a white sock with black and white saddle shoes on. Her grandmother taught her how to sew and she carried this skill into her young adulthood as she sashayed her talented black and white wardrobe around Harlem streets. Since she didn't earn much money as a poet and dancer, she made white wedding dresses for the women of NYC and they even requested her to weave in black lace or black ribbon in the wedding dresses because they knew that was her signature. So she made wedding dresses as her main income and wrote poetry and danced on the side. Her dancing costumes consisted of sassy black and white with black fishnet leggings and white frames of shoes with black heels. She would sometimes wear black and white feathers in her thick black curly hair as she danced and it all was sending a social message about being black and passing for white. The ladies of either the white upper class or the ladies of the black bourgeois loved her wedding dress designs that they personally promoted her poetry and helped her advertise her dancing on Harlem stages. Although this would expose Natasha to jealous white women and she had to be careful with her blooming local Harlem fame. Besides the inner and outward storms that were brewing just beneath the surface of Natasha's life she continued to wear her creative wardrobe with pride. She wore black and white pearls on the same string and the necklace seemed to be a message of the oyster, where the mother of pearl grows in dark blue ocean waters.

The making of the wedding dresses was going well for Natasha but, at her own personal level, she still had the financial status of a struggling artist during the post Harlem Renaissance. She stitched each wedding dress with diligent labor and weaving black lace into the dresses was her signature. The wedding dress business was just a small personal business in order to make ends meet while she still wrote poetry and danced. She used silk and satin, lace and cotton. Her fingers were always at work with the wedding dresses for both white women and black women. She earned her living with grace even though she had to count her pennies and keep them close to her vest for she wasn't rich. She took measuring tape and measured ladies from around all kinds of shapes of bodies and she stitched each dress accordingly. It was like making satin dresses for bodies of fruit that reflected womankind of the 1920s. Although she had to be careful with dealing with so many ladies because not every woman is a true friend and especially if it involves business like Natasha's wedding dress making business. There were so many dark clouds slowly moving above Natasha for she was meeting all kinds of women and she had to be cautious because of this. There were ladies in cream-colored double-breasted suit tops and large-brimmed hats on. There were ladies with green eyes like tiger cats and there were ladies with curled-up blond curls and ladies with hair pulled back into buns. Some ladies looked in long mirrors and oohed and awed while fitting into Natasha's treasures and there were ladies that looked into the mirror and melted with emotion at the pretty white wedding dresses with the black lace sewn into them. But with all these ladies cooing and oohing at Natasha's masterpieces, one of them was at least bound to turn on Natasha. For Natasha just wasn't a dress maker she was a mixed race woman with a mission in life. Her mother had wrongfully been put into Lunacy asylums and this made her poetry and prose different from most people in Harlem. Just as her dresses and her poetry and her dancing was magic in front of onlookers and admirers so was her life at best. So while making wedding dresses for dozens and dozens of women throughout the city one of them was going to steal from Natasha because she saw how bright Natasha's star hung like a fat yellow halo all around Harlem. Although Natasha did not see it coming nor did she think about it happening in the first place. She started to see signs of thievery in the early stages but it was still too soon to tell what would follow. She made her wedding dresses and stitched with her hands beneath lamp light and the light of the bulb glowed softly into her nights as she closed like a man-eating plant at the twilight.

Chapter 5

As the green glossy palmed-leaves of plants soaked up the diaphanous rays of the sunlight, the aliens hidden within the light's shadow wasn't enough, for they had to report back to the Alien Fellowship about the company she kept and the expense it would cost her. There were just too many women coming and going in and out of Natasha's life because of her wedding dress business. And the aliens knew this and had to find ways to hinder creativity theft because black Americans had come a long way since the ending of the Civil War and they didn't want the black artists, most particularly Natasha, to be stolen from. So they pulled together their artistic moments in a black Renaissance task force to try and hinder a white woman from stealing the creative ideas of Natasha. The black Persian cat served as a witness and as support but could not hold back a white woman who was taking a keen liking to Natasha's creative power. This woman had more money than Natasha and had more support than Natasha. Even though Natasha worked hard on making the wedding dresses, she still lived at the poverty level because she bought the most expensive materials for her dresses but charged her clients at a lower price because she was being generous and fair. Furthermore, even though her wedding dress business took off the ground running by word of mouth, she still was a struggling poet and dancer, despite being recognized by the Harlem Renaissance. So when it came to flourishing her creativity and fame it was like she hit the asphalt each time because of a lack of support. Her poetry had spoken for itself and there was a vulture at every turn she took when it came time to promote herself and her poetry and dancing. The aliens on the artistic task force knew this and they had to come up with ways to billow out Natasha's artistry without it being engulfed in flame by a theft from a white woman. So as they shimmered in the noon light as plants sitting on Natasha's window seals they sent up the flame of the sun's light from the plant's palms as a prayer up and into the Universe for the sake of Natasha's life. The black cat would prance around Natasha's living room as ladies walked in and out of it as they came to get fitted for their wedding dresses. The cat listened, as the alien he was, to the chatter and the conversation of the ladies around Natasha. And, as space's communications transmitters picked up on what the cat saw, it would restore the information in the solar panels to one day better the creativity of Natasha. The task force knew they had a challenge on their hands as it wasn't easy to intervene with white thievery since it had so much power since the slavery days. The alien task force had to figure out how to harness Natasha's art and at the same time fight the centuries of white supremacy that was always just a short distance away from Natasha and other black artists. The aliens used their communication receptors and solar panels on their satellites to pick up on the artistic thefts that were taking place in Natasha's life and to the rest of blacks in the Harlem area. Their goal was to help Natasha recognize what was happening to her so that she could fight on a platform based on peace and justice.

So the aliens used their space technology to help communicate with Natasha through her dreams at night as she slept. They would be abstract dreams like abstract paintings and not direct messaging from the Alien fellowship. And so Natasha dreamt as if she were running and then flying to get away from someone on the ground. She saw herself flying between trees and then down again on her feet and then she would repeat the pattern of flying between trees. And the message sent in this dream was the message from the aliens that something was amiss in her life if she felt she had to fly to get away from someone or something. It also meant that while flying she was transforming into other realms like the alien world. The alien artistic task force weaved dreams in Natasha's sleep like a spider would a web. They came to her in her dreams as different types of animals telling her in a discreet way that her creativity would be put to the test. One night she had a dream of killer whales' fins swimming in rising ocean water. The meaning of this dream was that the rising water meant something in her life would go afoul but at the same time she had protection from the Universe because dreaming of killer whales meant just that. She dreamt of mysterious beings with red velvet robes on with deer antlers among snow. These beings were the aliens silently communicating with each other over Natasha's fate. She dreamt of snakes swerving and swerving and hissing and this was also the aliens communicating with Natasha as well. The snake seemed to be saying that something toxic was to arise in her life and that she should take action. She also dreamt of a pack of wolves howling up at night and their black and white fur was the same coat of hair as her black Persian cat which spoke of friendship and guidance. She dreamt of flying above the ocean while she looked down and saw a great white shark. This dream meant a future of fortune and seeing the shark meant she was at her creative peak. She dreamt of an alligator being cut which meant rising above bullies and toxic relationships. The aliens intercepting the dreams of Natasha was their master work of communication for they learned it through centuries of traveling back and forth in space and time. While it seems unusual for alien life to overtake the dream of Natasha, it is what they had to do in the name of finding justice for Natasha. Their web grew and grew and her night thoughts stuck to it and the stickiness kept her close to the alien's vests. They knew they had to cultivate her dreams as a communication tool, on their part, because it's what they had to do in the name of warning and alarm of the creative theft of Natasha. They spoke to her through all the images in her dreams while she slept although it was all discreet and their conversation with her was top secret.

As the morning sun would snake its way into Natasha's room, it was a reminder that night was over and that the dreams she had were messages from space above. As sunlight also hit the plants sitting in windows it was also a letter from the aliens. And the message was that there would be a theft of Natasha's creativity and life. The alien also possessed people as Natasha walked down Harlem streets, and they would pause and glare at her with eyes full of warning. It was all that the Alien fellowship could do to warn Natasha of a white woman plagiarizing her life. Their messages to Natasha twinkled in the stars at night as Natasha gazed up at the night sky. They always came to her in her dreams at night in abstract form. The aliens would also communicate through Natasha's friends as she sat with them for coffee or tea either in her kitchen or in Harlem cafes. These friends of Natasha's spoke the words of wisdom, which came from alien souls, about white women stealing the creative ideas of black women. These conversations took place in front of steam coming off of tea and coffee and the steam was like a warning smoke to Natasha and given by the Alien fellowship. The steam from hot water in fine china cups would curl up into the air and send out whispers in Natasha's ears in an abstract way. The steam was like the clouds in the sky holding water until it rained and the pouring down rain would also be a message to Natasha about her doomed future if she wasn't keen on listening to all the obscured messages from the Alien fellowship. When passersby would hesitate and look at Natasha instead would get frightened because she was not yet tapped into the alien messaging of her soul. Her cat would wave to her with one paw trying to explain to her that something wasn't right. The cat would wag its tail as the people on the street glared at Natasha with warning filled in their eyes. The cat in all his secrets tried to be the best witness to Natasha's life and the best witness to the people looking at Natasha on the street. And the steam from the hot water in china cups was a soothing warning to not stress Natasha but to awaken her just a little about what was to come. Natasha would sit at tea parties with her legs crossed with fine white gloves on and in black lace dresses and stare at the steam going up into the atmosphere she presently took up and would admire the communication from space.

Chapter 6

The messaging also came from a black preacher in a historically black church in Harlem one Sunday morning. The preacher warned the congregation of the deceitful beauty of snow that while it may look pretty at the same time it is cold and dirty quickly. The preacher's voice bounced off the church walls like an echo from the Alien fellowship that was now taking heed in Natasha's life. The brick walls stood firm in their acquaintance with the preacher's voice and it was like the soul of Natasha as she sat and listened to the preacher preach about the downfalls of snow. The preacher went on to say that while snow may look good covering the landscapes and roads there is also ice beneath it that can be like a danger if not careful with it. Snow is the same color as the clouds in that the clouds can always burst with pride and there will be a snow storm. Snow storms are unpredictable and leave frost competing with warm summer rain storms. Snow on warm winter days is like impotence and the white flakes can dissipate in mid-air, all the while leaving slippery wet residue. Snow can be compared to humanity's cries and pain because it is like the cold where no sight of the sun seems to want to screech through when all the sky is bleak and empty. The preacher went on to say that one should never be let down by the coldness and bareness of snow for there is always plentiness on the other side which is spring. Snow banks and snow caves, hail storms and heavy fat snowflakes can trick the soul with its artificial beauty. So never let snow know who you are as you walk through it or stomp through it. Even if you do stomp through the snow, your echoes will get lost in the complete whiteness but your footsteps will leave a trail and remind you of where you have been. Don't believe that snow is the voice of angels because it is white. Snow will lure you into cold places and force you to reach deep within yourself where it is dark and warm. For this snow has done something right but when one is blindfolded by its fake beauty it always wins the soul over. One must take back what the snow has taken with its majestic depleting magic and find themselves questioning snow's motive. Snow is the devil in disguise and wearing a white cloak as if he were some sort of winter god but don't believe the hype. Mud and grit and grime can live both on top of snow and beneath it so beware of the messaging it gives when browned at the edges like a dying flower. Snow also tries to compete with the heat of the sun but nothing can beat the power of the sun. Snow will never be life giving like the yellow from the sun curtailing snow's life as if a mercy killing took place. Believe in the gods that circle the miracle of the sun because the snow is the opposite and will kill with its promise of beauty and kindness.

Credit: The African American Baptist Church on 16th and Chrisitian in Philadelphia

Chapter 7

Cecilia Johnson was a white aristocratic lady via NYC Broadway production. Her husband owned all of Broadway in the city all throughout the early 1900s and into the 1920s. Ms. Johnson had known about Natasha's dress making through mutual friends and by word of mouth. She also became familiar with Natasha's life story around tea gatherings among ladies of the upper class NYC. Cecilia Johnson also was a writer herself, she wrote plays for her husband's Broadway shows. So she decided to write a play based on Natasha's life, but without giving her any credit for it. She planned on paraphrasing Natasha's poetry and would insert Natasha's dance style in the play. The Alien fellowship saw this particular theft coming and they had tried to warn Natasha of the devastating blows of thievery of her life. And to repeat, they came to Natasha as the steam coming off of tea at tea parties, and they came to her through the black preacher who preached about the deceitfulness of snow. Although all the warning seemed to only sink into Natasha's subconscious and not her immediate conscious. Cecilia Johnson, although she may have been working hard on her script for a play, she was also stealing from Natasha's life because of jealousy. She drummed up three different acts that would best suit a popular Broadway show that would rake in a lot of money from people who really wanted to come to the show. She wrote in the mornings among steaming coffee while the sun sat in pink at her kitchen window. She slaved away on the play and chiseled it into a fine piece of work even though she was stealing from Natasha's life story. While Natasha's dress making business was revolving the money back into the dress making materials, Ms. Johnson worked with millions and had twice the support in the community than Natasha did. While Natasha shouted out her poetry about passing for white on Harlem streets, Cecilia Johnson was sitting at her typewriter within her luxurious life circumstances and was writing the story of a poor Harlem girl who grew up to be a Harlem stage dancer and street poet. In all Johnson's upper class privileged wellbeing she was writing as if Natasha's soul was her own. As she wrote the stolen story she thought she felt Natasha's adversity as her own pain but her own circumstances showed the world the contrary. It was these psychological thefts of Natasha's heart and life that would one day prove to be a complete emotional hardship for Natasha.

The first scene in Cecilia Johnson's play opened with Natasha's character dancing on the streets of Harlem in black and white dance attire. The female character is dancing by a light pole and twirls around and around it until onlookers clap for her. She dances in different styles like Fred Astaire and ballet styles. She dances without music playing but the crowd's cheers seem to give rhythm to the dancer's steps. The dancer suddenly stops and says to the crowd that she is dancing for her black mother who is currently impacted by several different hospitalizations and that these incarcerations were happening to many blacks after the Civil War was over. The dancer dances on and stops at times to give light to her life story. The dancer said to the street crowd that her black grandfather was away fighting in World War II and that her black grandmother raised her in black Harlem even though she passes for white because of the genes of her Irish American father. The dancer suddenly starts to dance again, and repeats the pattern of telling stories of passing for white while being an active member of Harlem's Renaissance. As the dancer slows down her step she stops completely and says she wants to recite a poem about being black but in a white body. She says I am as black as space and the stars from my limbs stretch out to be the lady in the night skies. The light of the stars gives away my father's heritage to me, but within me I am African American as thick as the blackest color molasses there are. As a mulatto woman that passes for white, I dare hold up my guard at ignorance and dance under a Harlem sky for the sake of the rest of my people. I am the lone black ballerina in the streets and New York City dares try to eat me up, but I then take it by tail and turn the situation around in my own favor. As she speaks poetry on a Harlem street corner to onlookers, she dances and repeats the pattern of stopping dancing and recites her poetry with a wide open mouth. The street crowd claps to the rhythm of her spoken word and also to her dance steps. The crowd repeats what she says in terms of her poetry and she starts to dance as the crowd's repeated spoken rhythm startles her back into a dance routine. She goes on to say poetically that while her black mother has been held against her will, the morality and the meaning of the Great Migration will bring her back to her true self. The steps my mother takes down those barren hospital walls is a step closer to understanding the meaning of the Universe and in the end it will be mine to behold and to crown my mother in her misfortune turned to riches and diamonds. I speak of the injustices done to my mother and I fight like the soldier my black grandfather was. I will not stop dancing until I see that my black mother has seen justice and written in her name with her own blood onto the sidewalks deep down in Harlem.

Chapter 8

After the opening scene of Natasha's life with her dancing in the streets it goes right into a flashback scene. This scene entailed her grandfather in a situation in World War II. Her grandfather is sitting around a table playing cards with his soldier peers when one of them chirped up that they should each go around and give an estimation and prediction of their unforeseen grandchildren's futures. Natasha's grandfather says he predicts his grandchild will face much adversity in the world but will get through it creatively. He also predicts that because his family came from the Great Migration that this fact will help his grandchild when pursuing her dreams of becoming a great stage entertainer. All of a sudden, as the soldiers sat around the table, a burst of light shone through the window. The soldiers looked at the light all perplexed but suddenly the light went away. The soldiers sat around and wondered where the burst of light came from. One thought it was a divine message from God, while another thought it was "truth" from the skies as the grandfather spoke of his grandchild. Another soldier thought it was the bursting of clouds after something similar to a rain storm like when a rainbow appears afterwards. Another soldier thought it was a message from a system of Greek gods from the sun, since the light seemed to come from the sun. The grandfather said he found it interesting that a funnel of light busted through the window as he spoke of the future of a grandchild and that it probably meant that he was on point about his prophecy. The soldiers went on to say what they thought would be the fate of their grandchildren and they continued to play cards. One soldier said he thought his grandchild would experience polo but this would make them very creative since losing one basic skill can sharpen another. Another soldier thought that his grandchild would be a political leader and "move mountains" with change and passion. All the soldiers noticed when there was no funnel of light as the rest of the soldiers spoke, only when the grandfather spoke. So they started to predict the way this was, and so they came up with the assumption that only the grandfather's vision of his grandchild was accurate. But they still were mystified as to where the light came from and started to say they believed that there may actually be a god. One soldier opened his wallet and threw down a wad of cash and made a bet about where the light came from. So another soldier told him to put his money away because there was no real prediction of where the light actually came from and because of this the light coming through the window was priceless. So the soldier put his money back in his wallet and said that was a right observation and that he shouldn't have thought to put money down on the table in a guessing game over a funnel of light that was divine and priceless.

After the tunnel of light dissipated on Cecilia Johnson's stage, there remained a dancing Natasha in a black tutu like a ballerina. She raised her feet upward like in a ballerina's stance and swung out her arms like a swan. She started to recite her poem called "black grace" as she danced with pointed-up toes and her arms flapped like a swan's wing would. In between dance moves, she again recited her poem: Black grace is not curtailed by the wind, but made by it and the wind lifts up blackness like it does autumn leaves and carries black grace to places unknown. Black grace is always in the air because of this, it does not fail it only grows with both time and the very wind that carries black grace. Mine is the cherry blossom leaf that fell off a Japanese tree-but Japan is just a metaphor for me – like Hiroshima I go pale from breathing in the gas of hatred. And I become like a white swan that once was a black swan gliding on top of ocean storms. Black grace is even carried through stormy ocean winds and in night skies I can see my future carry me through the foreseen catastrophes. As yellow billows out from the noon day sun, its light is actually at my beck and call, as I ask for it to help when I dance. The yellowness dances around black grace and lifts up its limbs as dancers of Harlem do their thing. And as the authoritarian man in the sky looks down at me, the wind will continue to carry my black grace to places he cannot see. For these places hide my black grace from authority so bitter I can feel the wind protecting me. Black grace has been ahead of its time. It's been around the ancient pyramids as the wind carried it there. Black grace has seen the ownership of Africa – the oldest inhabited continent of the world. Black grace has been galvanized upward to the sky as the wind rose up ancient black ghosts straight out of Africa. For this reason, black grace is almost older than the planet itself, for black grace is the same color as space. I wear black ballerina attire as I dance at this moment, for black grace is never too far from me. Black grace stings like a bee when the bee is fluttering among roses and the red petals fall like blood drops at the bee's stings. Black grace can ride out any storm and fly the ocean long like a wandering albatross and the arctic tern. What my black grace does for me, is that it sings to me when I feel all alone and there is no one there for me. My black grace dresses me up in courage in times of need and war. My black grace knows me better than I know myself and others as well. Black grace is the thing that carries me through when my life seems to be limping. With that, Natasha's character bows gracefully to the onlooking crowd while only a funnel of light shows on her body that is dressed in a ballerina's black attire.

As the black grace scene came to an end and the curtains closed on a dancing Natasha, the curtains reopened with a flashback scene. The setting was in World War II, with Natasha's grandfather fighting in the trenches. He is holding his gun and having a conversation with a fellow soldier. As there are blasts in the air from the war, Natasha's grandfather kneels down in the trenches and speaks of his pregnant daughter. He tells his fellow soldier that his daughter is pregnant in one of those Lunacy hospitals and that local NYC police put her there for rebelling in the streets. He went on to say that they thought she was crazy by walking the streets and yelling and she even took off her shirt in protest one day while she was protesting in the streets. The grandfather went on to say that his daughter is his only baby and that he couldn't wait for her newborn to arrive. As war blasts went on and on around them in the trenches Natasha's grandfather lamented to his soldiers concerning his daughter's condition. He went on to say that he didn't believe that she was really crazy although she may be a little on the crazy side, at first glance, because it's in her African DNA to fight political circumstances. He went on to say that Natasha's mother has a "fighting spirit" like him and that his being in the war reflects, in part, his daughter's behavior in the streets. He went on to say of his daughter, she fights a bloody war like I do, and if that makes her crazy then so be it. As the grandfather and the other soldiers keep hiding in the trenches, fires and blood orange colors from guns and smoke snake up into the air around them. Blasts keep going off, and panzers zoom by as the soldiers take cover in the trenches of war. The grandfather continues to speak of his only daughter and says that while he is the minority as a black man in the war, his daughter carries this legacy within her, even in the mental hospitals as she walks the barren white walls that enclose her. The grandfather speaks of his "baby" because she is his only child. Rockets and soldiers with long guns pass by the trenches, it's as if the opposition can't even see Natasha's grandfather hiding in the dug up piece of ground the encapsulates him and his soldiers like a tomb. The grandfather says, when I get out of this war I am going back to NYC to drag my daughter out of the Lunacy ward so that her and her baby can have a normal birth and life and not be locked away like a criminal – and that she is not. He goes on to say that even though his daughter is still alive, he sees her as an angel out in the battlefields or in the war nurses' faces, he essentially sees her in every good deed of the war.

After the World War II scene with Natasha's grandfather in the trenches, Cecilia Johnson's play veered toward another flashback with Natasha's mother protesting in NYC streets. With the protesting in the streets, the police come and shuffle away Natasha's mother. She is seen being boarded into an ambulance because she was screaming in the streets. Although from her core, she was protesting police putting African Americans in hospitals after the Civil War. And here she was being hauled off to a hospital, somewhere in the city, because she was outspoken but her body would shake with screaming and the police thought there might be something wrong with her. Natasha's mother was also a very beautiful black woman and tested high on the IQ test. The play showed an attractive black woman screaming in the city streets with police and ambulance shuffling her away in their big wagon. This scene also shows Natasha's mother haggard and in the hospital yelling at nurses and doctors. She told them that she was only defending her rights, since the war had been won by the Northern part of the country, and she went to tell them that here she was in the North and was being held against her will. A once beautiful black woman had turned to look stressed and disheveled on stage while in the hospital scene. The scene turns back to the streets of NY with people going about their business while Natasha's mother is fighting for her freedom in the hospital. To make things worse, she does things to get attention in the hospital like tying a sheet around her neck. This prompts the doctors to order restraints on her, and the scene shows a once beautiful black woman all restrained in hospital shackles. She cries out in solitary confinement that she is once again experiencing the pain of her black relatives and ancestors by being put in hospital chains. The circumstances of the hospital break Natasha's mother's spirit and it makes her look both in penury, beaten down almost tortured when once she was considered the most beautiful black woman of her time. The stage was all white and sterile looking for this scene and women dressed in white dresses and nurse's hats shuffle on Cecilia Johnson's stage as if they are defiant ghosts dismissing the cries of Natasha's mother. The scene shows a spotlight on a chained up black woman as she continues to scream for her freedom and her life. All the while doctors in white coats and nurses in white dresses have their backs turned on her on the side of the stage that eventually fades out to black and the only thing left to see is Natasha's mother in hospital restraints almost speaking in the tongues of Africans who have lost their lives on the high seas as they were brought over to be slaves. Natasha's mother is seen shouting that the Civil War is supposed to be over! The Civil War is supposed to be over, yet here I am in your prison and in your chains and for what reasons!

After the hospital scene, Cecilia Johnson's play moved toward a poem read by the main female character. The poem was about passing for white and having the heavy burden of a white parent's genes. This scene was another giveaway that Johnson picked up on Natasha's street poetry as she recited her poems about passing for white and having a white father and black mother. Natasha had originally invoked the imagery of great big palm leaves that mask her away from the sun, and this is why she has lost her color. On Cecilia Johnson's stage there are giant palm leaves hovering over the leading black female character as a round light above the stage represents the sun. Natasha's character starts to recite the poem about having a white father and a black mother and passing for white. She stands in the middle of the stage as the giant green palm leaves stand above her. The light from the stage light hits the palm leaves and leaves shadowy shapes in the space where Natasha's character is standing on stage. She starts to recite the poem about how the palm leaves mask my heritage and the sun, and I am left a ghost color where I almost disappear and dissipate into non-existence since people cannot see my black side. I lament at this clear facade that I have to wear because even the sun has a hard time getting to me. The yellow rays shoot down from the sun's sphere and hit palm leaves, leaving the leaves a glossy green while I suffer from being in the shade. Even when the sun has baked me a golden brown, people still don't believe me that I'm black and proud. The killer whales in the ocean are like me, they are black and white and they are friendly giants of the waters – but when messed with they can tell you as they leap up out of the water and slam back down on it as a warning. This is also like me, the killer whale with both my black and white attire will warn even the Universe to take notice of me. The green palms shade me on the ground whereas the waters carry me to where I need to go to get back my black grace. This is because the water does not discriminate. Its deep depth makes it that way and my old friend the sun hits the surface of the water with its rays and the water goes back and forth like a welcoming soldier with the sun's grace. Whereas I see the great bodies of water beneath the moon because both the water and the moon never hate on people like me, it's because both of them made people like me. And as for the great big palm leaves in jungles they can shrivel up and dry in the middle of the sun's volcanic ash. And when that happens I will burst like red lava showing by African side, always burning and churning, always on fire at the stake of forbidden time.

The stage went black with curtains falling on the female character reciting poetry about passing for white. Suddenly the stage lit up again with another flashback scene with Natasha's mother in the hospital. This time the beautiful, but haggard looking, black woman is very round in her stomach, as she is pregnant, as the white walls of the hospital surround her. She is talking to a nurse and asks why she has to be here while pregnant. And the nurse replies to her that it is to keep her baby safe. The woman replies back to the nurse that she wouldn't hurt her unborn baby and that keeping her against her will while pregnant was like some kind of social ill. The black woman goes on to explain that many of her people are impacted by hospitalizations and that is why she herself is in the hospital. She goes on to say that is why I was protesting in the streets, to see the day blacks are free from all forms of incarceration including hospitalizations. The nurse says to her, be thankful they didn't throw you in jail where you could be assaulted with words or even punches. The black pregnant woman says that she feels like this hospital is a prison, but with the facade of helping me. I do not need medical help, what I need is my freedom to be black, woman and proud. The nurse says that it is not a facade and that a little bit of medical treatment wouldn't hurt anyone. The nurse claims, you may not see it but I am on your side. I can sway the doctor into thinking that you really need to be here instead of just shipping you off to jail. The black pregnant woman says she doesn't know what is worse, being thrown in a hospital for protesting in the streets or being thrown in jail, it's all the same to me. The nurse leaves the room and the black woman is left alone with a round light on her. She stands up and you can see that she is nearly full term pregnant. The round light disappears, and a broader, wider light appears on stage. Large windows are behind the pregnant woman and there are palm leaf plants at the windows. The pregnant woman walks over to the windows and stares out them like a moment of peace and quiet. She looks down at her pregnant stomach and says to her baby, see baby look at the world, surely your future is brighter than mine. May you conquer hate with your wit and grace and create many good things for this tired and worn out world. The world is your pearl, your mask and then your grave. May complete universal angels guide you away from that mask and be who you were born to be. A fighting spirit in the name of your fighting mother who has fought injustice most days of her life. May you always fight and strive with great will power and wear the world's pearls around your neck like a crown.

As the scene fades out, another fades in with the dancing female character beneath a round light. She is in a red ballerina's outfit and her feet are pointed upward as she flaps her wings outwardly like a bird. She says to the crowd, as you may all know my black mother carried me the whole nine months in a mental hospital. I was just a sprout at first until I grew into a fatter fetus and took up the space inside my black mother's womb. Her black belly that was fat and round with me looked like the moon at night time. The placid little waves of the Hudson River lapped onward as my mother was made to stay in the institution with me. In my childhood I never saw swans swimming the Hudson River, but they may have when my black mother was pregnant with me and held against her will. Birds would dip toward the river's surface as my black mother looked out the institution's windows while pregnant with me. The world must have been a complete injustice and on fire to her while pregnant with me. The Civil War was over in 1865, and the start of putting blacks in hospitals began and continued all the way up until the present day, the 1920s. It's been about 80 years of suffering in the institution and a lot of it goes unchecked and unrecognized. So here I am dancing in red and at the same time spinning the tale of my imprisoned black mother. This red represents a fire, a blaze so hot one could not possibly be near me. For my fire rages like red storms do in space and the debris from that storm echoes out into the Universe and it spells out my name. And I am Natasha Brown the poet and the ballerina and dancing in the shadow and the grace of my beautiful but doomed black mother. The world should be on fire like this pretty red dress that flares out and makes a bold statement. And as those birds dipped down toward the Hudson's surface they were taking back flight instead of drowning in the water. And they did this as my beautiful black mother sat in an institution while pregnant with me. And perhaps black crows circled the institution like a palace or a doomed kingdom and they watched the situation like a hawk would. And then one realizes that those same crows that circled the institution were the same birds that dropped into the river but then took flight like a commercial jet would off a runway but in this case

83

the Hudson River's surface.

Natasha's character continues to dance across the stage and make huge leaps in the air as part of her dancing routine. The music is playing fast classical music as she dances and dances and spins and spins. The music slows down and then speeds up like the way a storm would. With every rip curl of the music, Natasha's body sways to the beat never missing a step. As the music goes faster, this is when Natasha spins continuously across the entire stage and there is lightning and thunder heard as part of the music's makeup. Then the music stops and Natasha's character tiptoes to the center of the stage and leans forward while bent down, and puts one arm out as if she is reaching for the audience. All of the sudden the music speeds up again and Natasha's character does magical leaps in the air, all the while she flares her arms out like a swan would. The onlooking crowd is darkened by the blackness of the theater all the while Natasha's dancing character twirls and whirls around and around like the ballerina she is. The music slows down and now Natasha's back side is facing the audience as she crosses one leg over the other and motions her arms up and down like a classic swan character. As she looks to the left while with her legs crossed over and flapping her arms, the music picks up again and then Natasha's character dances frantically around and around on the stage as a cyclone is seen on the projected wall behind her. Then suddenly a rainbow appears and rain is heard while the music is playing softly this time. Natasha's character is on her tiptoes this time and gliding one foot before the other across the entire stage. Then she spins around with her full body and puts one leg up in the air behind her, and she has her arm out reaching toward the audience again with the other arms gracefully at her side. She seems to be like an ice queen or a figure skater at the Olympics but she is dancing on her toes to the rhythm of classical music with storm sounds weaved into it. As the projected picture on the wall dissipates, Natasha and the music are left alone. The music speeds up again and Natasha's dancing character folds both arms to her chest and spins with her legs crossed again across the stage. And then all of the sudden she comes to a standstill with no music playing and she is left alone in the middle of a round light in the middle of the stage. There is only blackness left and it is hugging the parameters of the light that surrounds the dancer. She puts both hands on her hips and looks up toward the right side of the stage. All is quiet, and there is no more music. Then suddenly Natasha says to the onlooking crowd, this is me, black and proud, even though the palm leaves mask the sun and leaves me pale. The light fades out.

The red velvet curtains fall on the dancer, and then they open again with a flashback scene with the black pregnant woman in the institution. She is being transported from the mental hospital to the medical hospital to give birth. Two nurses are on either side of the pregnant woman as they escort her to the ambulance. The ambulance leaves the institution's grounds. The scene fades out like blackness, then the stage lights back up with light with a woman panting in labor with nurses and doctors around her. The baby is born and the mother asks to hold the baby as they have taken the baby away right at the moment of birth. So they bring the baby back and hand the baby to the mother. The nurses take guard over the woman with the baby with one nurse on either side of the bed. The woman holding the baby says she will name the baby girl Pearl Natasha. The mother looks down at the baby and says, I am naming you Pearl because natural pearls are imperfect in shape and size just like us, for we are here and we are not perfect. The nurse asks to take the baby to the doctor and

85

the mother asks the nurse, what will happen to my baby if I have to go back to the institution? The nurse told the mother that the baby would be safe either in foster care or with relatives. The mother shouts out to the staff, what have I done to deserve such treatment? You make me sit the entire duration of my pregnancy in a loony bin and then you plan on taking my baby from me! This is supposed to be my happy day, giving birth for crying out loud! The nurse hands the baby to the doctor, and the doctor says that despite the baby being African American the baby is very pale like a slice of day moon. The baby's cries pierce the stage and bounce off the red velvet curtains and onto the audience. The mother says that her baby can go with her mother in Harlem because that was the best place for the baby since being around black folks in Harlem would help in the raising of the baby to be a good honest person. Then the mother says, when I am finally released I am going to wear a pretty dress with a string of pearls with cream-colored heels. I am going to take back everything that has been taken from me including my baby and my freedom to be black! The doctor and the two nurses scuffle off stage and the mother is left in the middle of the stage with a single light on her. I would like to take my father's gun from the war and blast it off like fireworks but only up into the air. For I will not stoop down to their level and I hope my baby does the same and never stoops down to any type of evil even when that evil has taken everything from you, including your life your child, and your freedom.

The scene fades out as usual, and then another scene opens up with a joyous celebration on the streets of Harlem. Since Pearl's mother gave her mother guardianship of Pearl, the Morning Heights neighborhood was full of joy and very proud. The people of Harlem are seen dancing on stage as if it were Harlem streets.

They were clapping and dancing and singing lyrics like, you'll be a star someday, little sister, you'll rock the moon with your circumstances! There were men in brown and tan suits with brown fedora hats clapping, dancing and singing. There were ladies in flapper fringe dresses with long strings of pearls around their necks to pay tribute to Pearl the new baby. They dance in a circle around the stage and throw their arms up into the air and say, we won, we won we have our little Pearl in our Harlem arms! The government did not take our Pearl away, they left her with her blood grandmother and that is unusual. They started to sing Civil Rights songs like "We Shall Overcome" and "Black is the Color of my True Love's Hair". The dancing continues on stage as if they are on Harlem streets and they sing out loud about how Pearl is their little star and little sister. Then they dance in unison like an orchestrated musical would and the ladies beaded fringes flying up and out into the air, while the men take off their fedoras and throw them up into the air and catch them. The ladies heels make a loud tap on the wooden stage as if they were tap dancing and they are singing about how God blessed baby Pearl to come home to Harlem. The men are dancing in sync with the ladies and they sing in their monotone voices how great it is that Pearl was with blood family and not adopted out. They are still dancing and they sing to little Pearl about how the Great Migration got them where they were and that the Harlem festival of the arts was all their time to shine. With arms outstretched in front of them and mouths opened round they continue to sing to the beat of a newborn baby girl and her circumstances of winning over bureaucracy. The Harlem dancers shuffle and kick back and forth their legs as if they were on a treadmill and they continue to sing the greatness of the situation of how little Pearl won by being with her true blood grandmother. And so the dancers gathered back into a dancing circle and sang about how the grandfather was one of the only black men in the war and that when he came home he would be awarded with a sweet little offspring, a baby girl named Pearl. The dancers formed back into a line with the men on one side and the ladies on the other and as the ladies' fringes continued to throw up into the air and the men's fedoras twisted upward as well, they stopped suddenly and took a bow forward in front of the audience.

The stage goes black again, and then curtains reopen with the ballerina in the middle. Slowly from the ceiling the representation of the planets falls from strings. The ballerina slowly glides across the stage and then gets on her tiptoes and starts to go into a dance routine. On the screen behind her is a visual of space, all the while the planets are tingling just above the ballerina as she swoons across the stage. She is wearing pink with pink ballerina shoes on and she has gold stars as decoration tied in with her hair. The classical music that is playing is heavy and fast and seems to bounce off each planet that is hanging from the ceiling above the dancer. The ballerina stops and pauses on her tiptoes and starts to recite a poem of hers. She says with elegance, the planets are mine if only I look from within and see my lost innocence. Space will one day ordain me princess of the blackened space skies and I will live in peace eternally. The moon as my guidance will never be too far from me, for I have been its obedient student. With the old saying that it is your oyster, I blossom from a similar shell as the oyster. For I am Pearl that was raised by the people of Harlem and the planets have surely lined up in the realm and in the name of Harlem. The thunder claps so loudly in the space skies because of what happened to my mother. The storms in space are not happy with the way Earth authorities treated my mother and therefore the storms will not stop in space as the planets stand still and keep the storms at bay. The planets are all lined up and stand still within their peace even as space has a subtle anger because of what happened to my mother. The classical music starts again and the ballerina starts to twirl and take bows across the stage. She raises up on her tiptoes again and positions up her hips and puts her arms in the air as if she were an eagle. She brings her arms back down slowly and gracefully and squats her legs downward and then jumps back up and turns left on the stage and starts to do three leaps in a row. With each leap she lands softly on her feet. She then does several spins from where she landed and end back up on the middle of the stage. She then goes underneath the first planet and says this is mercury, and then she says all the planets names one after the other as she glides beneath them. On her tiptoes she toddles back to the middle of the stage and takes a bow. The black space sky behind her disappears while the planets slowly go back up to where they came from. The only thing that is left is a circle of light on the ballerina in her bowing position.

The planets lift back up as the stage goes back to black. Suddenly there is a yellow and orange light spotlight on the dancer and it represents the sunset. Pearl stretches her arms up into the air and is standing on her toes. The yellow orange light follows Pearl around as she dances and sashays across the stage. This is the final scene of Cecilia Johnson's play on the life of Natasha. Pearl continues to flap her arms up and down as she swoons and dashes on the stage. She is wearing a yellow dress with an orange ribbon tied around her waist. Her outfit also represents the sunset as all things end for the day as the sun goes down and goes to sleep. And like everything goes to sleep when the sun goes down, the play has to come to an end. Pearl is also wearing yellow ballerina shoes and the yellow on her feet complement the light that is falling on Pearl. Pearl hesitates in her dancing and recites one last poem. She says she is a dove flying toward the sunset despite being black but passing for white. She goes on to say that the sun closes its big yellow eye as the world rolls back into black. That blackness is my final destiny as I am trying to get to my black grandfather who died in the war. Blackness is also my destiny because I try to get to my black family members every day since the light of the high noon sun has been hidden by an eclipse and makes me pale like fog in misty mornings. Pearl continues to dance to the slowed down classical music as she also slowly glides one leg before the other in a dark ballerina routine. Her yellow and orange outfit reflect in the theater's light that is bouncing off of her gracefully like liquid light falling on any given object. The red velvet curtains are patiently waiting at the wings of the stage as their velvety red projects Pearl's soul aflame with both hope and fury. And even though Cecilia Johnson's play is a forgery of Natasha's life without Natasha's permission, the Cecilia Johnson stage does a dark justice to her life anyway. Pearl continues to spin and twirl around and around to the beat of the music and she suddenly lifts her tiptoes once again and slightly dashes across the stage while flapping her arms like a subtle dove in a peace after a storm. This peace was like the quiet grave of her black grandfather as all the yellows and the oranges project off onto the audience like a quiet wake. Pearl's pale complexion is wavering in the yellow light as her blatantly jet black hair gives a mysterious contrast to the yellow light and the yellow she is wearing. She takes three big leaps back to the center of the stage and does a demi-pointe and then does a pirouette as she finishes and then takes a bow.

Chapter 9

As Cecilia Johnson's Broadway play started on the stage in downtown New York City, the Alien fellowship knew they had a problem on their hands. This being said, they could tell by the history of Earth's patterns of wars, in particular, but in this case a theft of a black woman's life via Broadway by a wealthy white woman. So the alien artistic task force was called into action by the Nation. They knew all about Cecilia Johnson's connections to Natasha Brown via tea parties and the wedding dress making business. The alien artistic task force's goal was to hinder Natasha from acting out once she found out about the plagiarism of her life on the Broadway stage. The Alien fellowship told the alien task force to let Natasha act in her own way, to let things unfold as a consequence, because if done this way Natasha's soul would grow strong and be enriched. The task force was also told to not let anything of a violent nature erupt among the two women and to hinder violence if it were to come up. The Alien fellowship told the artistic task force to come to Natasha in the usual subtle ways like through nature and even through light that would be shining through her afternoon or morning windows. The task force was also told to go into their usual physical form but to be invisible if anything drastic should arise between Natasha and Cecilia. Their physical form also entailed angel wings because the task force from space was essentially guardian angels from a Universal Utopia from somewhere else from up in space. The Alien fellowship told the artistic task force to fly with their wings and to be in full alien body if anything dangerous should pend against Natasha. They were also told to enter into Earth as birds, since birds had similar wings to their own wings and that the bird would serve as a spaceship on Earth without Earth realizing it since birds belonged there. The alien in charge of the Alien fellowship and the Alien King and Queen also advised the artistic task force to communicate with Natasha's cat at the ladies' tea parties so that Natasha may be aware, astute and on guard. The aliens in the artistic task force were also told to be the reflection in the cat's eyes as Natasha held it and talked to it or looked at it. They were to communicate with Natasha in every discreet way possible without being found out. These subtle and mysterious messages, according to the aliens in charge, would be like a gift to Natasha from the Alien fellowship and from space as well. Finally, the king and queen alongside the Alien fellowship told the artistic alien task force to remember where they came from and where they could be if found out by Earthling authorities. We would be persecuted and experience a similar pain to that of Natasha Brown and her black family so always keep this in mind when abstractly communicating with her and protecting her like the angels we are.

One morning, as the sun rose quietly in the NYC skies, Natasha was drinking her morning coffee with the cat sitting below her at the kitchen table. As the steam from the coffee curled up into the air, Natasha looked down in the cat's eyes. And then she saw her own face's reflection in his eyes. The cat's eyes served as a mirror for Natasha as she looked in them and she became perplexed. The cat started to meow at her and put one paw up into the air as if to motion something to her. She shook the cat's paw and went about drinking her coffee. Outside her kitchen window, the morning sun rose and rose until it couldn't go any higher into the late morning skies. The messaging from both the sunrise and the cat were hidden communication styles in order to warn Natasha of Cecilia Johnson's play regarding her life and it was done so without Natasha's permission. The yellow, pink and orange rays from the morning sun and the cat's meows were there to tell Natasha of the plagiarism of her life. The cat pounced up onto all four of its legs and started to circle around the kitchen table while Natasha still drank her morning coffee. as she could see her own reflection in her cat's eyes, she would also see her reflection in the 5 a.m. black slate of the glass of her kitchen window. Two reflections of her face seemed to be telling Natasha to take a closer look at herself and the direction her life had taken since Cecilia Johnson's Broadway play concerning her life. Even though Natasha just saw her face's reflection in the eyes of her own cat or in the coffee she didn't think much of it. She was just enjoying the morning sunrise and her morning in which the sunrise was saying so much to her she didn't even realize it. The cat at this point was circling the kitchen floor and turning its head toward Natasha as if to get her attention. Natasha asked the cat why it was making circles around her and what was it trying to tell her? Natasha was starting to get a bit startled by the cat's behavior and she was also starting to slowly realize that her cat may be trying to communicate with her. This scared her a little bit, because the cat never seemed so alert as he was now. The cat's alertness alarmed Natasha but she didn't know what to think or what action to take because of it. She just sat there, in her warning state, and just kept looking at the pink and orange late morning sky. And even though she was sitting in her kitchen where she was surrounded by walls, it was like the yellowness and orange of the sky was wrapping around her. She hadn't known at this point that her soul belonged to the colors of the sunrise since she was the child of a mistreated black woman and she hadn't known that this is why the sunrise was rising for her, or setting for her.

The colors of the skies belonged to Natasha, and to repeat, because of the way her African American mother was treated after the Civil War and also after the Great Migration. If the morning skies turned from pink to orange or from orange to blue it was because the angels in the skies were painting the different colors just for Natasha. If the morning sky went into the afternoon sky, and the afternoon sky went into the twilight sky, it was changing just for Natasha. And as far as the sky knew Natasha was its owner and she held the spiritual keys to the sky alone. When the twilight sky turned into the night sky, the night sky would resemble space and all just for Natasha. If there was a warning in the forecast about the skies opening up into a storm, it was a warning to Natasha and Natasha alone. If there was going to be a tornado formulating in the graying skies, it was a message to Natasha that something was amiss in her life. If it rained or there was lightning or thunder it would be a reflection of Natasha's wrath. Although whether the skies were a pretty color or if they were turning dark like into a storm it was all in a good cause, for the life of Natasha. The skies didn't treat her like a prophet per se, it was just that her mother had experienced the great pain of the whole Universe if not the Earth alone and that is why the sky belonged to Natasha. And as the planets sat just above Earth's skies they were also forming a line when the time came for Natasha to see what had happened with her life being plagiarized on Broadway. But the sky could only warn Natasha so much of what was happening, for Natasha had to see for herself what had been done with her life and without her permission. As Natasha glanced out windows and looked up at the sky, she had no clue that she would one day be the inheritor of that sky and the keeper of it. Looking at the sky made her so oblivious like she would rock shut like an oyster closing its shell. She was heavy with blindness when it came to what belonged to her, for she still had not known there was a paranormal presence in her life. She could look into the eyes of her cat all the days long and even see her face there, but still it would take a while for her to figure out that the sky belonged to her and that she had alien angels helping her every step of the way. When the sky would shut its eye in the nights so did Natasha for she still had not yet found out about Cecilia Johnson's play concerning her life. When the sky would open back up in the morning and its peachy colors would swirl about with pink and blue it was a wakeup call to Natasha. And as the sky would hit high noon it was a warning sign to Natasha. And as the sky went back to sleep at night, so did Natasha until one day the sky would open up with a brewing storm.

Chapter 10

And then there were positive signs everywhere telling Natasha that despite her circumstances she was loved by the Universe. Even though the alien artistic task force was working hard to show Natasha that her life had been that extraordinary enough to be plagiarized, the planets were also speaking to her as well as they were lining up. As the planets lined up it was seemingly for Natasha since her black mother had experienced so much hardship. When the planets were in a complete line people in the streets of Harlem were subconsciously picking up on Natasha's poetry and prose and therefore they were saying bits and pieces of her work out loud in street conversations. Natasha would be sitting at a coffee shop with her cat on her shoulders and then all of a sudden she would hear someone repeat a poem of hers that she had not yet released to the public. Even though there was negativity going on with Cecilia Johnson's great plagiarism of Natasha's life there was a positive sign in random street people repeating Natasha's unpublished work because it showed the magic of the planets in line. If Natasha wrote about how "yellow fog" surrounded the planet Venus, she would hear someone at a coffee shop talking about yellow fog for no apparent reason. Another instance is when a young woman on the street was making paintings of the gases that make up the planets, and this was another poem of Natasha's. People would be talking about Broadway and how the characters were complete with names and people would be talking about being Irish American and this was also in Natasha's writing. Although Natasha and her cat would just sit and listen as her work would somehow bubble up in random conversation, she thought to just ignore it but deep down inside she knew something magical was happening. She didn't know where it came from or why it was happening. All that she knew was that she heard her unpublished work being repeated on the streets and at coffee cafes. Despite a storm brewing just beneath the surface of Natasha's life, all these positive repeats of her words and poetry were a clear indication that the planets were lining up and lining up just for her. Just like the colors of the skies belonged to Natasha, so did the planets in their complete orbits and positions in the planet lineup. But in the end the real question was put down before the council of all space. Did space as a whole belong to Natasha and just how far would the gods of space go to reckon with what was done to Natasha's mother and would they be willing to give some of their power to Natasha?

Other days were not so fortunate as people repeated the content of Natasha's work on the streets. For there were days when there were real actual storms that hit Harlem and the rest of the city. If a tropical storm hit the southern part of the country, the residue from that storm would subside into Harlem. On Natasha's day the sky would go gray and dark blue to almost black when there was warning of a storm coming through. The alien task force didn't want to use this type of messaging to get across to Natasha that something was wrong. But they had to turn the bright blue summer skies like a fortune wheel so that they could somehow speak to the soul of Natasha. Natasha was also daring in the weather, she would walk the city streets with her cat on her shoulders and holding a big black umbrella. She would seek shelter in store doors when she thought it would go from just rain to lightning and thunder. And when there was a blizzard she would wear snow boots and walk alongside the icy snow banks so that she could embrace the winter where the winter felt so close to her own spirit that was now pending. The artistic alien task force also would use the snow to communicate with Natasha. They knew that she felt challenged by the snow and so they would make the snow firm on the banks and actually make it snow on pinkish winter afternoons. When Natasha was young she used to like to make snow angels with a big blue bulky snow suit on. And while she would make the snow angels she would look up into the sky and see the day moon looming over her as if it were her mother loving her in a different type of way. Messaging through weather was not just confined to Harlem, if Natasha picked up a newspaper and saw that there were tornadoes in the Midwest and hurricanes in Florida, these were also warning signs about what Cecilia Johnson had done to Natasha's life and without her permission. The grainy black and white print of newspapers with stories of storms on was like a letter in the mail to Natasha. Besides the positivity of the people of Harlem subconsciously picking up on Natasha's unreleased pose, the negative messaging was never too far away from her. But the artistic alien task force didn't mean any harm to Natasha, by any means, they were only figuratively talking to her through the weather and through the great alien spirit projected onto Natasha that she must act in a peaceful way at the plagiarism of her very life. And Natasha's moods were also contributors in the change of weather. For Natasha's power was so strong that when hurricanes formulated upward from the tropical seas and when the sky went dark it was all unknowing because of the personal power of Natasha and all because of the pain of her African mother.

Chapter 11

On a summer afternoon as Natasha sat out on the balcony of her Harlem residency, the sun's heat and rays circulated and hugged her limbs like a warm hug. Natasha was drinking sweet southern iced tea with a male friend from the streets of Harlem. As they drank the southern sweet tea and bit into blueberry and orange scones, her friend told her about the Broadway play he had been to the night before. As the summer day ambience of cars honking and saxophone players and people walking by continued, her friend looked at her and said that the play resembled her life a lot. He started to break the play down into the acts and into bits and pieces and he said the title of the play was "Injustice Butterfly". He told her that the main protagonist was a lot like Natasha because the character was dancing in the Harlem streets and reciting poetry about passing for white just like Natasha did with her life. The taste of the sweet tea was now becoming unusual to Natasha as she felt like there was now a bad taste in her mouth. She didn't want to hear that a character on a current Broadway show was reciting poetry about passing for white in Harlem. At the news of this, her shoulders started to hunch over and she felt her heart drop. She also started to feel sick to the stomach and her soul started to ache. Natasha asked her male friend who was the author of the play? And he replied that it was a woman named Cecilia Johnson. Natasha's whole body shook for the moment and then sank into her chair. She started to panic and she wanted to throw her cup of southern iced tea out onto the road below her. She turned to her friend and said that she knew Cecilia Johnson through the network of her wedding dress making business. She said that she knew Johnson was well to do and was married to the man who currently owned Broadway. Natasha unwittingly asked her friend to tell her more of what was in the play. He said that the character's mother was incarcerated in an institution and that she had a baby girl in there named Pearl. He also told her about the grandfather in the trenches of World War II. This time Natasha stood up and threw her glass of tea down on the road and watched it smash. That thief! Natasha explained. Natasha went on to say that she knew something was amiss because her cat's unusual behavior and the weather seemed to be talking to her in an abstract way. I pick up on these type of things, easily, Natasha said. Natasha's panicking was now turning into fists that were punching the air. Her friend looked at her, and said, you have a case on your hands... As the high noon sun's waves curled around the sensual but furious Natasha, the heat was baking her like an oven until it set fire.

Despite finding out that her life had been copied on Broadway, Natasha still had tea parties to go to and she still had to continue her wedding dress making business. While she sat alone by a window that undulated the sun's light into her sewing room while she sewed dresses, she was on the verge of having a breakdown. As she nervously sewed and sewed the white silk fabric into a wedding masterpiece, she thought about her life and how she wasn't as rich or as well to do as Cecilia Johnson. And as the yellow from the sun projected onto the white fabric, Natasha continued to think about what had been taken from her. She thought of her mother who had suffered enough and of her successful grandfather who had brought the family out of the threats of poverty. She thought of her grandmother who had raised her to be aesthetic in the arts and she thought about how her beloved black Persian cat was always on her shoulders watching everything. Her whole entire life flashed before her like a bolt of intense lightning hitting the pavement. She felt like she was as powerful as that bolt of lightning but at the same time she also felt powerless. She thought to herself, how could a well-to-do white woman of the upper class of New York City society possibly understand black pain and most particularly her black family's black pain? As she was sewing the black lace into her signature wedding dresses she thought she, despite being affluently robbed by Broadway, had the upper hand because she was the one between the two women to have black blood pumping through her veins. She thought that Johnson as a white woman must have been jealous of black power and that is why she thought she had to steal from Natasha's life story. It didn't make sense to Natasha that a white woman of well means could possibly understand what it is like to be black if she wrote an entire script about it for Broadway. And despite the injustice that Natasha saw coming she continued her livelihood's craft of sewing together wedding dresses and selling them at a reasonable price. And the injustice she saw coming was actually going to the theater and watching the play unfold unjustly before her eyes. She thought that if she ever went to see the play she would gag and be in a lot of emotional pain. The late afternoon sun sunk down faster and faster, as Natasha finished her sewing the yellow light was now turning to gray shadows on her wedding dresses.

Natasha took walks on the streets of Harlem during this difficult time of finding out that her life had been put on display on Broadway. And as she walked she saw people glaring at her with speakeasy eyes as if to tell her that they knew what was going on with her and Cecilia Johnson. She would be walking the crowded streets of Harlem and her fellow African Americans would wave to her from afar or smile and wink at her as they would pass her by. She always had her cat on her shoulders as she walked the streets of Harlem and her cat was, too, picking up on the glares of people as they passed them by. When she would buy fruits and veggies at the street market, vendors would also look at her with speakeasy eyes. And they would say to her, aren't you the one that dances and recites poetry at the same time? As she would walk away from the vendors she would be full of wonder inside her head, that had now become like a planet. And as she would be walking, black brothers would say to her, hey there, little sister, how are you? It was as if space was now coming to a conclusion with the wonderment in the street people's eyes as they looked at her. And of course the artistic alien task force would embody these street people as they looked onward on her. Their kind glares were like a warning from the alien task force that her life was coming undone at the seams because of the poverty she was in but also because of the great theft that had taken place. Groups of black men standing on street corners gave her speakeasy eyes as well or groups of blacks playing musical bands with horns and saxophones would stop and hesitate and look at her as she walked by them. Black children playing hopscotch and jumping rope would laugh and smile at her as she would pass them by as well. It seemed that everywhere she went she was being regarded by everyone on the streets of Harlem. In large bakery windows she could see the bakers stop what they were doing and wave at her as their large cast iron black oven in the background was symbolic of the heat building up inside of her. The artistic alien task force was there in everyone's smiles and hopeful glares. They were the force behind the acknowledging energy of Natasha on the streets of

Harlem. And the alien task force never hesitated in their work in finding justice for Natasha. They were in every wink and nod, smile and song played on the streets of Harlem. They were persistent within their own beings when it came to helping and even saving Natasha from the great theft of her life. By the sweat of their brow and the alien blood pumping from their alien hearts they never gave up on Natasha. That is why when she walked the Harlem streets she saw their faces incognito and they were always there.

Chapter 12

Natasha had a fitting to do one afternoon with a lady who was a part of Natasha's circle of friends. The woman, named Petal, was over at Natasha's place and was getting ready to try on the wedding gown that Natasha had made for her. Natasha pulled out the wedding dress from the walk in closets and took off the plastic covering. She then held up the dress to Petal and asked her if she liked it and was she ready to try it on. The dress was white with black lace trimming on the bottom. It also had black lace sewed into the top part of the bust of the dress. The lady took off her current dress and was standing in a silk slip in front of Natasha. Natasha unzipped the dress from the back and had Petal with one leg at a time get into the dress. With all four of their hands they managed to slide the dress up past Petal's breasts. Petal turned forward to look into the long mirror while Natasha zipped up the dress. Petal said that she loved the dress, especially the black lace that was incorporated into it. And then Petal said to Natasha, you know I saw Injustice Butterfly on Broadway last night and it heavily resembled your life story. Natasha put her hand on her forehead and said, I know, I know all about it. Petal said to Natasha, it's like Cecilia Johnson is putting your personal business out there for everyone to see. She even put a black woman in an institution in the play and all the ladies at tea time know about what happened to your mama. Natasha said to Petal that fitting dresses on several ladies and all the ladies going in and out of her place because of the dress business is more than likely how Cecilia got a hold of information on her life. Petal patted down her new dress with the inside of her palms and sighed. As Petal was touching her new gown she said that ladies like to gossip about each other, when they should be friends and keep each other's information close to the vest. Natasha said to Petal that while it may seem she has her act together, her blood is boiling at a temperature that not even the sun could recognize. Petal said to Natasha, I would be angry if I were you, but also don't stoop down to her level and do anything stupid either. Natasha took a bottle of red wine out from her dresser drawers and then went to the kitchen to get two wine glasses. She brought the glasses back into the fitting room and said that they were going to have a toast. A toast to mine and my black family's life that has been good enough to be plagiarized and put on stage, and a toast to the lawyer that I will soon hire and a toast to my grandfather's gun from the war.

After the red wine toast Natasha and Petal gave to the black side of her family, Natasha was still together enough to go to a tea party she was invited to. At the party both white and black ladies were dressed in fancy attire with some ladies wearing hats with fishnet fashion over their faces. This gave them a dramatic look, like at a funeral. Ladies were also wearing ice blue, pink and yellow blazers. But Natasha was wearing a black sequin skirt with a white blazer on, showing her signature wardrobe of both black and white. As the ladies' heels made a clap clap on the cherry wooden floor and then sat down, the chatter began to snake up into the air. And despite the circumstances that Natasha was dealing with at the moment she was keeping a cool demeanor at the tea party. The china on the table decorated the room with white china cups with pink cherry blossoms curling up them. There were lemon scones and chocolates as well as coffee and tea kettles sitting on top of tables. Natasha who was wearing black lace gloves put the back of her hand to her forehead and sighed. The woman beside her asked what was wrong, and that's when Natasha explained to her about Injustice Butterfly, the play by Cecilia Johnson that had seemingly taken ideas from her life. This caught the attention of all the ladies as they all looked toward Natasha with stunning amazement in their placid eyes. Another lady spoke up and said that she knew Cecilia Johnson and said that Cecilia would never do anything like that. Natasha said in return, I didn't expect you to believe me – if you want to support evil go right ahead. The lady, with the yellow hat tilted on the side of her head with a yellow net covering her face, still stood her ground and said that Cecilia would never steal from anybody, especially from a black person. Natasha was starting to get fidgety and she felt she had to defend her theory that Cecilia Johnson had indeed stolen from her life and put it on display on Broadway. Natasha went on to say to the lady with the yellow fishnet covering her face that there has been a history of white people stealing from blacks whether it be industrial ideas or, in Natasha's case, creative content. The lady in the yellow hat still claimed that Cecilia wouldn't do such a thing, that she stood up for African Americans and that is evidenced in her work. Natasha said to her in return how could Cecilia possibly know what black pain is, furthermore how does she stand up for African Americans when she is stealing creative ideas from them? Natasha took off her black lace gloves and threw them down on the table top. Natasha then said to the lady with the yellow hat, I can't believe I'm still sitting here and still have tea time with you when all you want to do is call me delusional and stand up for a bigot! With that said, Natasha stood up and strode out of the kitchen, through the living room and then to the parlor where she then exited the door.

Chapter 13

Now the Alien Queen was no fool when it came to Natasha. She was a clairvoyant queen, at best, but she also knew by the history of white people stealing from blacks that she had, indeed, a pattern to track. Especially when it came to Natasha Brown and the great plagiarism of her life that was put on display on Broadway. So the Alien Queen set up a meeting with her artistic alien task force. On a spaceship that was traveling through space, the queen held a meeting in one of the rooms of the ship. While darkness and stars passed them by, the queen told the task force that she saw danger in Natasha's near future and that the task force was to help her but in a limited way. The queen ordered them to keep their identities close to their vests, but at the same time take the necessary actions when Natasha seems helpless and not in the right state of mind when she is under pressure. The queen also told them to stay inside Natasha's cat and remain her closest companion most certainly during this time of crisis and distress. The queen went on to say that while they would like to take hold of Natasha hundred percent because she is in pain, let her make her own decisions. Whatever choices they are or whatever happens then, she told the task force, then you take action that will help Natasha so that she doesn't hurt herself to the point of no return. The queen went on to say that they are only her guardian angels but we can only do so much to bail her out of trouble. Whatever Natasha chooses to do, you must at the same time let her deal with the consequences of those choices. For it is the pain of brave choices that will rebuild Natasha up. That is why we only interfere with limits and boundaries. The queen went on to tell the task force that, while they are to only keep Natasha's safety and best interest in mind, always remember your boundaries and let her make her own choices. Only under extreme circumstances do you make her decisions for her when she appears that she cannot decide for her own best interest. The queen went on to say that, in pain, Natasha will be able to grow to her fullest and utmost potential within her life and that is why there are limits within which the task force is to help her. While you let Natasha make her own choices you may be the alien angel that flaps your wings while you surround her. Give her your support, but not all of your intelligence. Let her make her own mistakes while at the same time she grows up from those mistakes. Just be her friend and only under crucial circumstances do you make decisions for her. The Alien Queen went on to tell the task force that, while an injustice happened to Natasha the great alien in the sun will continue to rise and set every morning and evening. Let the clouds move back as they will as if they were curtains in a play – the play that will play out when Natasha is finally the one in control. Let her ride her mistakes high in the noon day sky for I am a clairvoyant queen and I already see what she will decide and the mistakes that will make her strong in the end. She went on to tell the task force that their job was to only keep violence at a maximum distance away and to always make sure evil is kept at bay and at arm's length of Natasha as she makes her own choices. Be careful and always remember who you are – you are my artistic alien task force that was placed on the spiritual realm of Earth to protect Natasha because of how her mother was mistreated as a black woman. And always remember that fact when you remember your own utopian planets you come from and how you saw injustices subside and justice prevail at intervals. Never forget who you are as aliens to Earth but also as Universal beings that help humanity in a crisis and in this case it is through the female symbol of Natasha.

The artistic alien task force used the light of the stars in space to guide them back to Earth where they could help Natasha Brown in times of distress and crisis. They flew from their planets where they would sprout their angel wings and they became like their own spaceships. And space, to them, served as a conduit of hope and promise when they traveled through it to get to Natasha. There was nothing in space that would hinder them from doing the tasks that the Alien Queen wanted of them. And, with their angel wings, they could fly past all the planets that were now standing in a line with each other. They saluted each one as they passed them by and they were ready for their greatest challenge on Earth, which was the life of Natasha Brown. Of course, the light of the stars would guide them all the way through space as they traveled the speed of space's light. And they did not hesitate nor falter while trying to get to Natasha on Earth. They knew they were coming from a place similar to hers but now they carry an alien utopia within them as they travel to Natasha Brown. And there was nothing in space stopping them for this was a mission, a mission that space could have seen centuries beforehand. For Natasha Brown's life was incognito compared to the great Earthly queen, Cleopatra. And in the hidden meaning of Natasha, it was the history of space that built up her myth and her legend. For Natasha belonged to space just as she belonged to Earth. For she was the great soul teacher of the vastness of space and the victim of Earth's injustices. For this, she would be brought back by an alien utopian force that would see to it that water would break in space, for new life to begin again in Natasha's wake. And as the aliens traveled through space and time to get to Natasha they knew all of this, and they knew they had to uphold the phenomenon in both space and within themselves. So with their long wide angel wings like large birds they flew and they flew to get to Natasha. For she was their advisor, their victim, their motherly ship for all of the future of space. And as far as the alien task force could see, they saw in a grieving Natasha a life stolen, but a life given back to her by the grace of alien angels from space and the colors of Earth's morning skies. So they knew they had to get to her, to reinforce the warning that her life had been plagiarized and that she must take back what was taken from via peaceful solutions. They flew and they flew, through space, and they flapped their wide long wings as if the wings spoke while they flew, and just for Natasha. And as they traveled they were upholding the Alien Queen's clairvoyance and her mission to save the life of Natasha Brown and before it was too late for both space and herself. And they were flying to save space as well, because without Natasha Brown they knew they were nothing without the female force where that ocean like body breaks and the waters scatter and scramble to save space and the great Alien Queen which would one day be Natasha in her image.

Chapter 14

Natasha headed to her late grandfather's storage which still belonged to the family. In the backlands of Harlem and an isolated setting part of the city was her grandfather's storage of belongings from the war and the rest of his life. Notably, she rushed to the storage in the part of the city where female slaves had been buried beneath the very NYC streets that she walked on to get to her late grandfather's storage unit to retrieve his MI Garand rifle that he had used in defense of himself during the war. Natasha knew that his MI Garand rifle was to protect himself from the many predators of wartime and she thought that now it was time for her to use his same gun in defense of herself. She didn't believe in violence per se, it was just that her thinking was overcast by the thought of the symbolism of using her own grandfather's war gun against a woman who had stolen her life story and Natasha wanted her very name back because of it. She felt that not only had her life story been stolen but her name was taken with it. She knew she was on a figurative fire burning as she rushed one foot before the other to her grandfather's storage unit in an abandoned part of Harlem. She was breathing heavily as if heaviness were taking over the weight on her shoulders and down to the rest of her body. It was the heaviness of the feeling while almost running toward her grandfather's storage to get his gun from the war that was now taking over the entire situation. She embraced the heavy complications that were now invading her brain for she was deeply concerned and upset at the great theft that had taken place. As she approached the storage unit, which she had passed a lot of concrete empty buildings to get to, she unlocked the door and threw it open quickly. The darkness and the dust rushed in front of her eyes as if to say her grandfather's ghost was right there in front of her. She switched on the light, and saw army attire in greens and grays, military boots, medals awarded in shiny glossy gold and silver with purple and red and yellow ribbons holding them as they hung on the wall. She saw the Johnson rifle and the MI Garand rifle hanging from the wall. She didn't want to use the Johnson rifle because it was too close to Ms. Johnson's name and she didn't think there was any justice in the name "Johnson" rifle since the woman who stole from her had the same name as the gun. So she took down the most commonly used rifle by the army in the war, which was the MI Garand and brushed her hand along it. She thought to herself that the rifle would bring her justice since it belonged to her grandfather, her black mother's father. She thought that using the Garand would be like committing a justified crime against an enemy that stole her life and then put it on display on Broadway. When she held the gun in her hand she felt a sort of justice, but bloody justice, wash over her like a tidal wave emotion. And she held it in her hands. She knew she had come to a crossroads of making the most important choice of her life. She wanted to rock the MI Garand in her arms, but she knew she had no time for that. She was in a hurry to make the right decision and she knew it, but holding the Garand was like feeling close to her grandfather's ghost even though his ghost was telling her no and she could hear it in her ears like a physical phenomenon. His ghost was present, all right, but it was the most reluctant ghost in the Universe that took up the space of that very storage unit. Natasha felt both her fighting energy and her grandfather's energy that was now scolding her, but she stood her ground. It was the energy of a god-like force that was now consuming her grandfather's soul, spirit and ghost. There was nothing stopping his shield against his granddaughter and he would not put it down, for he knew she was in the wrong.

The artistic alien task force was on top of their game when they realized they had to go and defend Natasha as she made her way to Broadway, downtown NYC. She had the MI Garand in a duffel bag as she made her way to Cecilia Johnson's stage. If one could actually see the alien task force flying and flapping their angel wings in the air after Natasha, it would be a beautifying sight. The alien task force was flying fast and not faltering not even at one mishap. They raced after Natasha as she made foot to the Broadway theater. She was practically running with the duffel bag in hand and the alien task force was flying incognito behind her. As she ran through traffic and dodged people on sidewalks, the winged aliens were invisible at her back but the most important thing is that they were indeed there for her in this time of crisis. She made her way up the steps of the Lincoln Center's Vivian Beaumont Theatre on 65th street and entered the lobby. There she saw Cecilia Johnson's picture hanging on the wall. She took out the MI Garand and asked the people that were standing around to go get Cecilia Johnson. It was such a sight to see Natasha standing there as a 1940s woman and holding an assault rifle in her hands and asking for the owner of Broadway. The people around her panicked and fled, but the alien task force stepped up their protective measures of her and the people around her. One alien flapped his wings down gracefully at his side as he landed beside Natasha. And as he knocked the rifle out of her hands, and the gun fell to the floor, Natasha said, I wouldn't die in prison for you, Cecilia Johnson, my grandfather told me that violence is not the answer. And the alien that had knocked the MI Garand out of her arms repeated what she said about how violence is not the answer. The alien said to the other aliens to halt the police, and he went on to say, while someone safely gets this gun away from Natasha. The artistic alien task force formed a circle around Natasha as their wings gently flapped behind them. One of the aliens transformed himself into a human and gave the gun to Cecilia Johnson's husband who was now in the lobby. Police sirens were heard coming toward the theater as the aliens in the circle they formed stayed there until the police arrived. Suddenly the lobby was flooded with police officers and as they rushed toward Natasha all the aliens in the task force transmitted themselves into their bodies so that they could influence them and not shoot at Natasha. The police officer that came up to Natasha said to her that they were taking her to the hospital for evaluation and that she made the right decision by putting down the gun. Two police officers on either side of Natasha led her out to the paddy wagon and put her inside. Once inside the cop car they told her that she was not under arrest but that she was being committed to the mental hospital for an evaluation. As the patrol car pulled away from the theater, a flock of crows took flight into the open wide blue sky. Natasha is shaking and crying in the back seat and looks out the window and this time she sees an alien with wings wink at her as it disappears into thin air.

Chapter 15

The Alien Queen told her task force that they were going to lose control of Natasha Brown, but that they also had her future in their hands as well as a major American event that would happen in the 1980s and that would involve a child of Natasha's. The queen told the task force to let things unfold for Natasha as she went through the process of the institution while being evaluated at the same time. The queen told them that she already knew the outcome and that it was gloomy but at the same time it would build tough DNA in the future child of Natasha, and Natasha herself. The artistic task force pleaded with the queen to keep Natasha out of jail, if that was the case she was referring to, but she said she had no control over whatever was going to happen to Natasha due to the consequences of her offence. The queen went on to tell them that Natasha's life had already been riddled with mishaps and injustices, and that this newest situation would bring her to her knees and in prayer to the stars above her. For she is like a fallen star, the queen declared, in penury and jaded with all the time that has circulated in and around her life. The queen said that her father would back the decisions she made of Natasha Brown, even though she could see clearly what was going to happen to her. The queen went on to say that they had a bigger task at hand, which would involve a future child of Natasha's and a space mission from Earth. The queen said that this was the most important aspect of the life of Natasha's future child and herself and that they would do everything in their power to see that Earth's space mission was accomplished safely. The members of the artistic alien task force asked the queen exactly what she was talking about, and she replied that in time they would see what she can see of the future of the space mission on Earth and that they would have a role to play once it is launched. The queen assured them that this was a better mission to save and keep than keeping Natasha out of jail. Jail will make Natasha stronger in the end, and will instill ambition in her future child. While we are losing control over the situation with Natasha at present, I assure you that we will have a much bigger duty with her life about sixty years from now. The queen told them not to weep over Natasha, but to let her be held accountable for her own decision making and for her own soul's sake for it to grow from those decisions that she had made. The queen went on to tell the members that they will find out in time the fate of Natasha and the fate of Earth's space mission sixty years from now, which will have a direct link to Natasha's life, past and present.

While at the hospital in NYC, Natasha was evaluated and was deemed to stand fit to go to trial. A female sheriff in a light brown uniform with voluptuous curves read to Natasha her rights in the nurses' station and then she started to shackle her angles and cuff her wrists. While two sheriffs led her down the institution's hallway, other patients looked on at the scene of Natasha in shackles and with a sheriff on either side of her. They led her to the police car and put her in the back. A hospital staff member mouthed "good luck" to her as the patrol car drove away from the hospital. They drove her to the downtown prison which was the Manhattan detention center and once there she was led to the women's section. They had to put her on a watch in a big blue bulky prison dress in the suicide cell before they put her in general population because of the fragile state of mind that she was in. The correctional officer came up to her cell and looked through the bars at her, and told her she recognized her from reciting poetry on the Harlem streets. The guard went on to say that she was sorry that someone had copied her life for the stage, but it was still wrong to pull out a gun. With that the guard gave her a novel by W.E.B. Dubois, *The Soul of Black Folks*, and winked at her and said, see I know you well. Later the next morning she was put in the general population where the other ladies started to disparage her right away for the nature of her crime. It was like they were hazing her like in a sorority and soon after they were giving her oranges and milk from their breakfast trays. Natasha wrote a poem on a piece of prison scratch paper about how the lady sheriff was as broad as "a giant in the night horizon" when she picked her up at the hospital and brought her to the Manhattan detention center. One lady prisoner said that Natasha spoke like poetry coming out of her mouth. Other female inmates were asking for poetry from Natasha, but Natasha was too much in a thick heavy daze to write any kind of poetry on demand like that. While alone in her cell she would dance and sing like she did in Harlem streets or on the Harlem stages. She tried to make light of a heavy situation by singing in the cell and she knew it was just a matter of time when she would get her day in court and that justice would favor her side. The correctional officer that gave her the Dubois novel did sort of a justice for that slightest graceful gesture. It was like the justice system was going to align itself on her side and it was a sign that it was going to happen by the simple act of the guard giving her the Dubois novel. She didn't know how long it would take to see justice prevail in her corner but she had a gut feeling that she could win in court. It was like God was speaking to her somehow, and she heard the voice of God speaking to her heart because while she was damaged goods on the outside, her innocence was preserved on the inside. So she languished for days in the prison without a word, yet, from the courts and the dirty floor of her cell rose up dust and her very limbs became one with the brick that was holding her in.

Chapter 16

Natasha had a visitor while in the Manhattan detention center from a black Harlem lawyer. The lawyer stood tall and lean with a suit on and a red tie with blue dots. He sat down in front of Natasha and told her that she could possibly win the case that is currently against her because of a likely all black Harlem jury. In the air of the prison, the lawyer spoke with Natasha with grace, style and wit. He advised her not to automatically plead guilty just for a deal. He told her that he could fight on her behalf by bringing up the history of whites stealing creative content from blacks for a long time in the courtroom. He went on to tell her that while she is in the fight for her life, he also assured her that Harlem is a very black town and that would work in her favor. He told her that just because she is in a Manhattan jail doesn't mean that the trial can't be still in Harlem. The lawyer went into more creative language with Natasha when he told her to let the angels surround you while you are both incarcerated and in the courtroom. He asked her if she believed in the spiritual realm of angels helping humans, for he was both a preacher and a lawyer. He was also the same preacher who preached the sermon about not trusting in the snow. Natasha was sitting in his chapel when he gave the sermon about not trusting snow, and now here she was sitting in front of him as his legal client and her representation during a critical moment in her very life. He told her that she had the complete support of the community of Harlem and his black congregation. He also told her that blacks beyond Harlem would rally out in support of her because of the injustice of white people stealing from African Americans after an already adverse struggle with slavery. The lawyer also told her that everyone in Harlem can see what Cecilia Johnson did with her life on stage, because she grew up in Harlem with her black grandmother and everyone knows the family's story. He went on to tell her that not only does she have support from the community but she also has the support of public opinion as well, because it is definitely not politically correct to steal creative content from an African American, and an African American that is struggling at the margins of the poverty brackets. He kept reassuring her that she could win in court because of the fact that Harlem is heavily black and heavily artistic as well and that nobody in the black Harlem community would tolerate artistic thievery. He went on to say that the black community would especially not put up with stealing from a lone sister who grew up in Harlem with a black grandmother raising her on her own and overcoming adversity at the same time. He looked her straight in her eyes and told her that she had a great chance of beating the case and he promised her that she would see her day in court. He also told her that God speaks to him in mysterious ways and that God was telling him that something is going to touch the hearts of the jury. He told her not to weep in her cell for she will be a free woman in the matter of time, for God will see to it that the truth of Cecilia Johnson's own crime will come to light and the ultimate truth will prevail in the end.

As the morning sun rose on the Manhattan detention center, Natasha's cell door slid open. A guard came to her and told her that she was going to court. They cuffed her and put her in the prison vehicle and transported her to the courthouse. Once there she sat at the table with her Harlem attorney and he whispered to her that he got the battle won already by means of incorporating prayer and good faith in the people of Harlem and public opinion. The bailiff told the courtroom to "all rise" and everyone in the courtroom rose as the judge entered. As the judge sat down, so did the entire courtroom and the proceedings began. The prosecutor was the first attorney to speak on the matter, opening up their courtroom speech that Natasha used "malicious intent" to harm Cecilia Johnson out of jealousy. Natasha's attorney stood up and faced the jury and the rest of the courtroom. What are we currently in the middle of? he asked the courtroom. He went on to say that they were indeed in the middle of history in the making with the Great Migration and the New Negro Movement that has come from a place of conflict, violence and oppression of black people. He went on to say that we are also in the arts era of the Harlem Renaissance where formerly oppressed blacks have a chance to display their sophistication and creativity on both the political and artistic platform for the causes of social justice. But what will always be an interloper, and I hate to say it, but whites trying to or successfully stealing creative content from blacks and essentially the New Negro Movement. It happened to Esther Jones when she performed her "baby Esther" act at Harlem's Cotton Club and a white woman named Helen Kane notably stole Esther Jones' act and made it a white person's symbol in a global-like fashion. And when Cecilia Johnson's play came out, everyone on the streets of Harlem knew it was a replica and a steal of Natasha Brown's life. So essentially there is really no difference between the stealing of the "baby Esther" act by a white woman and now the robbery of Natasha Brown's life as a black woman but passing for white in Johnson's play "Injustice Butterfly". While Natasha was in the wrong for thinking that violence was the answer – it stopped there. Because she

121

ultimately changed her mind and put down the gun and ended up hurting no one. When you think of the violence that could have been, think of the violence that actually was – the torture of African Americans at the hands of slave masters and then the institutionalization of blacks after the Civil War. Natasha's mother was portrayed in the "Injustice Butterfly" play as being a victim of the institutionalization of black folks, but the real question is – what does Cecilia Johnson really know of black pain, if she is not black? Just south of the Mississippi River are located the states that experienced black pain the most and now a large migration movement to the Northern states is happening known as the Great Migration where many blacks flock like crows to the borders of freedom. And with them they carry that black pain, but it is being spun into a creative force right here in Harlem where blacks have finally found their day not just through post war legislation but through the arts as well. And for Cecilia Johnson to act like Natasha Brown's family's black pain is her own, and to furthermore make it popular in a universal way on the behalf of white folks is an injustice in itself.

Chapter 17

About fifty-five years after Natasha Brown was vindicated and found innocent, the Alien Princess who is the daughter of the Alien Queen took over the artistic alien task force which entailed helping Natasha with difficult life circumstances. The queen's father had owned an alien enterprise, in space, which was a factory that produced both spaceship and space shuttle technologies. And since the queen was born, the family's mission with Natasha's family on Earth was to make sure all the hardship was met with peaceful outcomes. Since the queen passed on, she passed her father's mission on helping not only Natasha, but Earth's space shuttle, the Challenger, to her daughter, who is the Alien Princess who now oversees Natasha and the Challenger on Earth. And she oversees the earthly space shuttle because Natasha's son is one of the astronauts who is to board the Challenger for when it is due to launch from Earth and straight into space. Natasha and her lawyer had a son together named Ocean Storm Shalom. He will be the only African American onboard the Challenger when it takes off. The Alien Princess calls together the new alien task force which will oversee the repairs of the Challenger by alien skill and mind mechanics. Since the princess grew up around a space shuttle factory that was owned by her alien grandfather, and because she was gifted with clairvoyant properties, she could clearly see that there was something wrong with one of the Challenger's auxiliary engines. So she called the Challenger task force and told them in a group meeting that a small round rubber ring in the second auxiliary engine would lose its seal and the Challenger will never make it out of Earth's realm, she claimed. She went on to explain that the space shuttle will dissipate in flame in mid-air, unless we step in and repair that second engine. She went on to say that her grandfather had been preparing for this day since the early 1900s, and he built a spaceship and space shuttle factory to make sure the perfect rubber ring for the second Challenger engine could endure an intense and powerful take-off. She told the task force to return to Earth and to take the rubber ring made by her grandfather's space factory and to replace it with the one that is already in the Challenger. This, she said, will keep all the astronauts safe and the space shuttle intact and it will live out its goal and mission. She also told them to be the space mechanics that represent all of space, and put their alien hearts into it. This will show that we help humanity in times of need and crisis, it shows that space has not only will power, but heart as well.

On January 28th, 1986, Natasha's son boarded the space shuttle the Challenger. He was the only African American onboard. There was also a teacher onboard, and before she boarded she gave a statement to the press about how incorporating a teacher in a space mission would encourage space travel in the future. As for the alien task force, they had already made the repairs of the second engine before the astronauts even boarded. All together there were seven astronauts to complete a mission in space which entailed flying there in Earth's space shuttle, the Challenger. The space shuttle was due to take off at around 11.35 a.m. on the morning of January 28th, 1986. Of course the alien task force was there overseeing the launching even though the astronauts had no clue they were there helping them. At Cape Canaveral Florida the space shuttle crew was preparing to launch. And in a single file line the space troopers boarded the Challenger with Natasha's son the first to board. A NASA overseer counted down from five, four, three, two, one and the spacecraft took off with the aliens now sprouting their wings from their backs and holding the space shuttle by its three auxiliary engines. The Alien Princess was watching the whole take-off from space and was pleasantly pleased by what she was seeing. The alien angels had helped the Challenger leave Earth's atmosphere straight into space. Once in space the space shuttle made its orbit around its own planet as the seven astronauts took notes on what they saw and made records from other spacecraft that were already in space. When their jobs as astronauts were done, the Challenger made a smooth and safe landing back on Earth. And as for Natasha's son, Ocean Storm Shalom, he lived to write the biography of both his black grandmother and his mother who both had faced so much adversity as black women during the Great Migration and the New Negro Movement and the wonderful thing was that he was still alive to write about it, and write about it poetically like his mother before him.

Epilogue

The poetic log of the Alien Princess, after the fact: I rode straight on the coattails of space's light after I rescued the Challenger and its flight. The light bent like a weeping willow beneath the sun, and I saw the light rays bend as it passed by the sun. There is nothing that can take away my power now, now that I have achieved my goal in space. There are space travelers that fly by the many thousands of moons that circulate the blackness and the stars; for fear is not for them, they are the homecomers of space so wide. I dug down deep into my alien heart and realized who I am, I am the Alien Queen's daughter with a plan. My plan is spacious like space's traveling light and not even gravity can pull me down. My power and my Challenger glory spreads throughout the galaxies and I, my friends, see to it that love and power swirl up like a forgiving snake into space's air. No theory about space holds water for me, for I am my alien mother's daughter that has dug so deep from within that I rule space as an alien female, a kin to humanity's womankind. From the bottom of my body and on up, I helped the Challenger survive because that was my assignment since my birth, my birth in space. For the roads in space are very long and wide and they lead to other galaxies so big and wise. I know that I am the alien female that can bend the light like the sun does, for the great ball of volcanic fire speaks to me like a god, and gives me feminine power in all space. After the Challenger's curtailed demise, I also saved the light that would have cried at the spacecraft's fate. If the shuttle would have died, in Earth's atmosphere, space would have shook with surprise and tears. For space is all the planet's land for all are welcome at the great star-speckled doors we all call space. And since the Challenger survived its journey out of Earth and into space, all must kneel at the fact of the peaceful triumph we call the shuttle's battle and win. May there always be that time, like the way space's light has time, the alien kin to Earth reaches for the justice of humanity. May the power of Earth's winds billow up into space and help us as well – in terms of understanding and the signing of the declaration of a peace treaty between the Aliens and the Earthlings. As I ride space throughout its trillions of years of history, mark this, my friends, that trillions of years knew of the Challenger and its challenge. For I the Alien Princess represent all space even as I travel and harness space's light, for I am also the great messenger that divides time as if to share. And the world we call space will be one world and I will no longer be called an alien but a being of the moons, a daughter of Jupiter, a sibling of everything and everyone all throughout space. But even so, I hold onto my power, as alienated as it may be. It is my lantern forward as I see all galaxies as my friends and peacekeepers. And from the light within me, I glow as space's princess that has saved the Challenger. And I am the great female of space, like a hidden ocean beneath waves my water breaks and the watery tomb breaks open as well and weaves throughout space. And my time will one day come to an end as I travel on the coattails of the power of light. And I can clearly see, like I saw the demise of the Challenger, that my alien death will be a calling forth, a throw back into the trillions years of space and time. My alien heart is what it is – a vessel of being female and the princess of all space; I rise to the occasion at my calling. And that calling is my lasting spirit that takes space by a pleasant surprise and I rise up like a space dawn and then space's atmosphere glows orange and yellow like the sun onto all the planets and then all the moon's orbits are one. The horizon of space is far off, one cannot even see it, not even me. For space is a Universe that is so big and wide not even God can see all of it or begin to understand it. I was once the whistle blower of the Challenger's fate, now I am the savior of spacecraft flight for the reasons of equality for all of space. I am also the princess, the ring benefactor of the union between the planets, and I am my mother's daughter, the Alien Queen that saw to it that peace prevails in black lives mattering on Earth.

After I saved the Challenger, I will take a long distance journey of all the galaxies. For wherever I am needed in the trillions of spaces that take up the blackness, here in space, I will be the one light in times of crisis. For I ride beneath the power of the light because it is more vast than me. My journey shall entail helping those galaxies in need even though they are made of light years so wide, I cannot even see. As I try to begin to even understand the relativity of this land here in space, I turn inward to find my alien heart there. And where I dwell is inside myself, where I have a history of saving Earth's space shuttle and humanity. And nothing in space, not even swallowing and drowning black holes would contradict me. As I travel forward into my journey and straight into galaxies unknown, I am on my alien family's mission to support and to help where it is needed. And oh, the missioning on the light years is so enduring even I get tired. But it is a good thing to wear out the soul from all this traveling. And as I travel I see that the rest of space is not dead, but full of life aglow. On my right I see snakes swirling and swirling and on my left I see a palette of reds and oranges as if it is a painting. I know there are space rocks that could fly in my way as I travel this land called space. I could ride on them like I ride on the coattails of light to see where I can go. And wherever I land, my alien grandfather would be proud of me. For where I land I will help with my alien gifts of intelligence. And when I get scared on my journey, I just look back at the history of my alien-kin past of saving lives on Earth and the Challenger. With this past and rapport in mind, I travel forward with faith and confidence. For what I will find in galaxies unknown to me will raise me to the challenge like the space shuttle, the Challenger. And I know that these galaxies will prove me not perfect but hopefully will cultivate my alien brain further into the depths of space and the rest of the alien kind. I will join my space family as I travel light years wide, and I will make sure I learn and grow. And I will always hold steadfast within my soul the day I saved the space shuttle and it glowed like a pulsating star in space's night sky. And as I travel onward, I carry the Challenger within me for the sake of luck and the love of all space because of it. And I know my time is limited and my time is never as much as the light years in space, but I will persist onward for the sake of making it even bigger than the Challenger. I know that I have the space gods on my side, because I saw them work within me when we stuck by the space shuttle's very side. And the gods harnessed my alien femaleness for the prize of the shuttle that made it to Earth's galaxy. And from this, I know that I have the support of the board of the gods here in space so wide. And with this knowledge I press forward straight into my journey as I look for my alien kind to help and to assist in times of crisis. And I, the Alien Princess, knows that even though the space gods are larger than me, they bow down to me as they use their intelligence through me. And I hear their calling me for the greater cause of me. And I felt their love of me even though my alien mother had moved many of Jupiter's moons. And then the sky in space will open up for me because of my past of saving the Challenger. And opportunity will knock for me as I travel the galaxies. For as far as I can see the stars will guide me as I take my journey. And their light will pulse for me as I seek their guidance and fortitude. For nothing can stop me after my fateful encounter with the Challenger.

I am on my way to space's largest galaxy which is Alcyoneus. I spread my wings and fly by the stars and swirling blackness. I know that I have a mission in mind. The biggest galaxy, with space in mind, has the most alien intelligence that I must find. For I know that the path there is long and I have passed many a moon in the width of grace so strongly. The land that we call space belongs to all and to all that includes the majesty of both humanity and aliens collectively. My alien wings flap upward like when our wings spread for the Challenger. I know the space gods will harness me with their knowledge of this mysterious Universe. I am the pivotal Alien Princess that is bound by space loyalty. I know that as I both float and fly in space's air, not even the weight of gravity can pull me down. For the roads are long and winding in space and my alien mother's spirit speaks to me along the way on this journey. I encounter rocks such as comets and asteroids along the way, but they are no bother unless they are directly coming for me and they are not. I have the history of my mother's circulating of Jupiter's moons for the magnetic reactions onto Earth and this shall guide me. For each moon's pull reflects my alien heart to oblige by the coming of the big alien utopia. And as I fly there I will eventually find what I am looking for. I come from the Jupiter monarchy, so peaceful – life and great nothing can take this away from me. So as I fly to the most spacious galaxy the gifts and the light from the stars will show me their pride in me. And as I look inward and as I look outward I see no catastrophe. Because the largest galaxy is hopeful with grace and intelligence, I cannot afford to lose sight of the intelligent kingdom of space. I will continue to spread my wings as if I was still carrying the fateful Challenger. Not only are the space roads long, they are deep with the inner workings of my alien soul and heart. I travel by the space gods' majestic workings on my wings that take flight. And I carry within me the light of hope from my alien grandfather's successful spacecraft factory. His work has been a blessing on my life and I will not resist it. It belongs to me and me alone. As I internalize the gracious gifts from my family's Enterprise, I know that my alien wings are just as worthy in any flight. And the moons my alien mother turned about will surely churn and burn on my life. And as I travel this space flight I am the pilot of my own body that is just as enduring as any spaceship. And so the roads are stretching out before me and the space storms are ever so near me but amongst the cyclones I press on. My grandfather's creations live inside me, they are embedded in my genes and they are weighed down within me like good gravity. So here I am, the Alien Princess on my mission of obtaining more intelligence. To assist planet Earth when they are in need and destitute. I am the pillar that stands in space's wind, I am the monument of space's historical pain. I know that pain will cultivate my alien brain. I keep flying on this journey, past light and past historical alien faults and glories. And as I fly I know that my alien history both personal and by the alien collective is not faltering in my step forward and beyond. This black deepness we call space is heavy and bound to the fact of helping each planet assist one another. And I am the gatekeeper of this fact. My family's alien monarchy gave me the key to great reason and the wisdom of knowing what to do in a crisis in space if that entails Earth. And so here I am still flying to my destiny after saving the space shuttle. And as I fly I carry my success within me so that I can further better my alien spirit. And oh my journey is so long and enduring but I keep going for the prize and the glory to better assist humanity and the rest of space.

On my way to my destiny, I stop alongside Earth's milky way galaxy. And an angel appeared to me, and she was full of glee: she said thank you for saving our dear Challenger and its journey. Her wings were as long and as wide as mine and fuller than the clouds upon Earth's surface. She had a porcelain face like a glass-faced doll and she was full of both hope and melancholy. She went on to tell me that I should remain safe throughout space as I travel so freely. She said that she is the guardian of Earth's gates and that all catastrophes would be washed away at the yearning for peace. She went on to say that while it is not easy, being the archangel of Earth's peace treaties is a pleasure and a challenge as well. We stood together side by side as space stood completely still. With our arms straight down and by our sides and our legs tangling downward toward gravity, we said our piece. Earth's archangel looked at me and said that she has seen many storms go through Earth's realm and through space as well. She said, this doesn't bother me for I am the shield of grace and I am full and proud. I told her that I have seen the future and the past of my Jupiter. And I told her that we have seen the faults in our grounds where quakes and other types of storms have shook our abode. I went on to say to her that there is time for these demises as well as time for harmony and justice as well. She said she knows where all of Earth's secrets lie when it comes to worldly leaders keeping historical facts so close to their vests. I told her, the same with Jupiter's former leaders, but they are gone now and now there is a utopia. As we gently flapped our wings as the peace between us passed us so graciously, space stood still with patience and her former glee. She went on to say that after the saving of the Challenger, Earth rejoiced and was now able to move forward at the pace of an incredible wind that dissipates and dips like a bird landing. The lady of Earth was very welcoming of me, she stood by my side even though there was the threat of gravity. We talked and we smiled and we looked at each other like we were in a mirror. Although my reflection onto her was like a spitting image and a double. At this point my soul bowed down within me and became still and subtle. Earth's angel regarded me because I saved her shuttle and now she recommends me to the highest court of this spacious space. She looked at me and said, you are the Alien Princess and I am the angel that sits on top of Earth and watches out for space savers like you. I know your traveling will bring you to a place of cultivation of your alien spirit and you represent your alien kin as you move forward toward space's dawn. The angel said I will glow my lights upon your traveling path so that you can see where you are going and we will work in cahoots like that. For you, dear Alien Princess, saved our shuttle and now we will pay it forward by lighting your path as you go forward. The angel went on to say, let no devil nor foe take either of us down while you go through this place called space. You are on your greatest mission yet, who knows who you will save as you linger onward toward the galaxies. The angel said that she was the peace winner of Earth's milky way and that she will guard it even though she may be in a historical disarray. She said to me, go forward anyway as I sit here on Earth even as everything is in dismay. Again, the angel said, thank you for saving our gracious Challenger, may the space gods be with you every day. With that first, her wings dissipated and then her body burned away, and I went along my journey happy that Earth is at least okay. As I fled away from the milky way, I saw other Earth angels flap their wings with love toward me, and they whispered upon the galaxy, thank you, thank you. And so again, I kept the Challenger within me as I flew off to my destiny. And even if I looked back at times with both melancholy and happiness the tears of my soul cried happily. For my tears are the tears of joy for the saving of Earth's space shuttle, and I look from within and find my joy there at helping it.

As I was passing by the Andromeda galaxy I came upon an alien patriarchy. He had antlers and jewels around his neck and eyes. He said that as I travel the galaxies one by one I will come upon many aliens next of kin who will speak to me. And I told him that this will give me wisdom for my journey as I oblige. He looked at me and clasped his hands together and then this is what he said to me: We here in this galaxy saw what you did for Earth's shuttle, and it has made us proud beyond belief. For we feel Earth's rupture like water waves coming toward us like a tidal and at times a hurricane. We have seen the overt oceans of planet Earth billow out its blues and greens of life, and we are pleased. We wish for Earth's bodies of water to live forever, so that humanity can thrive and survive any kind of weather. If you would have not saved the shuttle, it would have found a tomb in the Atlantic Ocean, and it would have given Earth a feeling of doom. While we are aliens to Earth kind, we are their upfloat like their very water. For we have helped them since the beginning of time and for trillions of years we thrived while they just came about like a blue marble pearl in space's wind. The world of space just does not belong to the alien kin, it belongs to all who are found here and to all who wish to be here. Space is long and deep and the many moons and planets that have water could assist humanity. Next time you see the Atlantic, look at your reflection in the water like a mirror so bright to aliens. And as you see the watery reflection of yourself, remember who you are and want to be. You are the Alien Princess from Jupiter who helped Earth in time of need. You carry this fact within you as you already know who you are because of this fact. Let Earth's oceans sway back and forth within your alien soul and you find yourself free. There comes a time when you must let Earth go so they can be free. Let them figure out the facts for themselves while using the great compass of the oceans wide that spread across the planet. Saving the space shuttle was enough help to carry them through for centuries to come. For we are not their saviors, my dear Alien Princess, for they must save themselves. They have all that they need in the great oceans, they can use the magic of their water to keep life bound like the trillions of years space has existed. And as you travel on, know that you will find knowledge in your alien next of kin and you hold that within you like the key to space's kingdom. For your mother's moons in Jupiter held deep and hidden oceans from within them like those moons knew who they were because of their hidden water and magic. You do the same, my dear princess, you hold the magic of water within you and you will glow like a star all throughout space. Let the waves of water rock like a boat back and forth upon the majesty of your soul and you will find yourself the beautiful alien you are – free and tied to the faith of space. Don't let your limits tie you to a stake in times of unrest, use adversity to your advantage to grow instead of faltering. You will always have your most successful memory of the saving of the Challenger so harness this as you journey onward. And always remember the water, the great Atlantic that you took over while our aliens held the Challenger in their very alien hands as it went forward up into space's land. That was enough on your part, my dear princess, now step down and let Earth shake your hand as you resign your post there. For Earth must figure out how to resolve future catastrophes for themselves. They are very capable because we see by evidence of the wisdom of the waters there. They just need to make the oceans on their planet the king of everything and let the ocean live figuratively in their souls. They will find a way out of their wars and injustices on their own if they just recognize the beauty of the water that is giving them life, firstly. So as you travel to our largest galaxy, may the great alien in the sun be with you always. May the sun's rays guide you back home when you have made it through your journey.

As I continued onward in my space journey, I stopped upon the Centaurus galaxy where I met with another alien. And this is what she said to me: Earth's mountains reach the skies like a sword sticking up from the ground. They symbolize strength and perseverance. As you travel on here in space carry within you Earth's mountains like a unity. You will feel blessed by the thought of the mountains for they represent your determination. Fly so high, sister Princess Alien, like the highest mountain Vinson Massif, Earth's highest elevated mountain. The rocky facades of the mountains crumble rocky like tears as they tumble downward. The snow that sits on their peaks is like ice crystals wavering out their reflections from the sky above as they sit there on top of the mountain. And as you travel forward go up like the Chimborazo Mountain in Ecuador, from where you are so high you will see the ground of Earth and then you will remember where your alien soul has been. Mountains play no games, if stuck on their rough-rocky sides they will show no mercy. This is a sign to not falter in your step the rest of your journey. Put your heart into every idea your alien brain comes up with and you will be kissed by space gods. And like the wide continent of Asia on Earth, spread your soul out likewise. The Saltoro Kangri Mountains in Asia are a reminder for you to walk the steps in space like you would on the side of the Asian mountain. And as you keep going here in space it is like traveling the perimeter of Mount Kilimanjaro that covers Nepal, China and the Tibetan border. Carry all of these Earthly places wherever you and your alien spirit will be enriched. For you, dear Alien Princess, are like a mountain yourself built by the fact that it took great courage to save the Challenger. The mountain of you will still be of the alien kind – always growing and learning and yearning for more. For it is the intelligence of space that we crave in crucial times of knowing. This is the gift of the alien brain and spirit that we bestow upon the rocky terrain of Earth. We glow our intelligence to Earth for the better like a benefactor from space. And then they grow to be as fast thinking as us because we know how to share. And as you spiritually climb Earth's mountains here in space, always remember where you come from and where you are going. And like the Cho Oyu Mountain in the Himalayas, be creative as you press onward in your climb in space like on the side of a mountain. Climbing a mountain is not easy and it takes a lot of determination, especially here in space. Because climbing space is like trying to understand what went wrong with any given spacecraft. You must know the tools when it comes time to fix a problem in space. You then must use those tools to chisel away at what all the galaxies have in store for you and your kind. Which is the alien kind that goes up the side of a mountain like the Jongsong Peak. And as you spread your alien angel wings toward the future, fly so high at the mountain peaks as you remember what you did for the Challenger. There comes a time when you must let go of the trillion years past of space and look from within when you educate yourself on the future of space – and what it can do for fateful spacecrafts like Earth's shuttle. Space is as big as a mother mountain. Her terrain will guide you where you need to go to get more intelligence for survival. As snow slides down the sides of mountains it calls your name, dear Alien Princess. You are the spaceship setter, you are the jet setter, so fly and fly accordingly. Know that your goodwill shall carry you to good peaceful places in space and beyond. And once you have looked from within yourself and found your successes there you will always remember how you changed the fate of the Challenger. Each figurative mountain that you will climb will reflect in the snow's surface at all the mountain's peaks. Your spirit will grow from there as you let your past climbing of space's mountains be the force that carries you home. And when you get home from your journey, put your alien wings down by your sides gently and say to your Jupiter family that your work has been done, surely for space's soul. For space will be satisfied by your glory because you had traveled it in search of more even after you saved the Challenger.

As I passed the Centaurus galaxy I came upon the next galaxy. An alien met with me there and this is what she said to me: Use Earth's Great Lakes like a compass. Their waters will give you not only strength from within but guidance as well. While you follow the pattern of space's stars, the surfaces of the Great Lakes undulate straight up into your being. And let the watery tombs be like a life giving force as well. Lake Superior that is in between both Europe and Asia is a very large lake that will send to you grace. As you fly you will not be actually above the lakes, but your spirit will be. Internalize the waters like an inner map so that you find your way to space's largest galaxy.

The Caspian Sea in Canada has got to be Earth's largest lake so remember this when you have memories of saving their shuttle. For your success and your joy of having saved the Challenger is just as big as the Caspian Sea. You are the gate's keeper here in space, your mother the Alien Queen saw to it. She moved the moons that had water on them for the sake of assisting planet Earth. May all the rest of space be blessed for this fact. And like hidden bodies of water in moons, find yourself there. For hidden waters in moons are like a soul encapsulated in a private time machine. The Great Slave Lake in Canada is not doomed because of its name, but it coagulates up the ghosts in its waters for the sake of peace and justice. And the Great Bear Lake in the Arctic Circle has much to offer you as you travel onward, let its compass show you where to go to get to space's biggest galaxy. And you will know all the water's preachings as you patiently listen to their callings. Lake Baikal in Russia will speak to you of the Russian language and will enrich your intellect as you go forward into space. And as you fly, think of the Great Lakes of Africa too. They have much to offer you because you saved not only the space shuttle but the continent of Africa too. Lake Malawi is located in Africa and the body of water is like a great African woman with her limbs and hips raised just above the surface. Let her guide you home when it is time, let her be your lantern in the forest. And Lake Victoria in Africa is like a queen as well. She speaks to you like your alien mother queen spoke to you. Be bound by her earthy and nature ties and you will see your own feminine spirit grow. And Lake Tanganyika is in Africa as well, spread your alien angel wings over this lake in a spiritual manner as you keep in mind space as well. And as you use your imagination here in space and alongside the Great Lakes of Earth may you be bound with the water with style and grace. For the waters in Jupiter's moon will break like a woman's and then you will see yourself an entirely different alien at the gates of the broken waters from the moons that glow fluorescent lights. And as you go forward straight into your flight carry the Great Lakes within you like a great commercial jet. Leave behind your past for the sake of the Alien future and for the coming of new knowledge of space aglow. For you will regard Earth and its Great Lakes and at the same time space as well. Let Jupiter's moons guide you to the place that you are going to for wisdom and growth. Mixing space's moons with the Great Lakes is a good idea when it comes to your travels. So travel onward into the night space skies and you will be better off for it. Let the waters carry you to your imagination while at the same time you dream in your rest. Your nightly dreams will come from the Great Lakes, for their waters will billow out into your alien brain as you sleep and settle like a bird ending its flight. And always remember the power of the Great Lakes, for they resemble your own power at best. And at large and not lastly, the Great Lakes of Earth will be your friend as you travel onward. Keep in mind the womanly limbs of the Great Lakes of Africa like Lake Victoria and Lake Malawi. They are like a symbol of the female on Earth and in space their waters will make sure of it. And their water lifts up and gives you light in the dark just as the stars here in space do the same.

As I was traveling through other galaxies to get to my main destiny, I came across yet another alien who had jewels and gems on their face and around their neck and this is what she said to me: follow the solar winds here in space for the comets captivate it so and will guide you where you need to go. Just as the Northern lights on Earth's arc north of the Alaska Range brighten the sky there, so the same with the northern lights here in this home we call space and time. For space is just not always blackened out, it has many colors like the northern lights. Follow the lights that bend and stretch by the sun's tides, and you will find yourself in many places so kind. The aurora borealis stretches out in front of you like a road to where you need to go. And the polar lights are the same but with a different name and you will see your soul glow in its peaceful wake. Always keep in mind as you travel through space that the aurora polaris is yours to keep so close to your accomplishment of saving Earth's shuttle. And your loving victory on Earth will be shared throughout space just as the northern lights are distributed among the planets. As you part your way from me, always remember this conversation as an alien gem and you will glow from within. For the northern lights both on Earth and throughout space speak to aliens alike as well as humanity. The lights are the strength that bonds both worlds and the solar winds surely are responsible for the traveling and the union of Earth and the rest of space. Just make sure that you always keep your alien heart open to what else is out there. For out there will bring you gifts of not only the northern lights afar but of brilliance. The stars are no match for what the solar winds can do for the northern lights here in space; they are just gatekeepers of the peace we call space. And as you find what you are looking for, always thank the northern lights for guiding you there. And as you travel forward, ride on the tails of the lights like it's the last of your life. And as you make it back home turn out the northern lights, figuratively, behind you as if a closure to your travels. But at the same time make peace with the northern lights and the winds that carry them for they are your great lantern in space so big. And as you settle back at home rest assured that the auroras guided you for your purpose so wise and so honorable. One day you yourself will be like a light in space that guides another to truth and peace. For, dear Alien Princess, you saved the Challenger and have made space's skies full of the northern lights as the comets fly by. Let all space kneel down and bow to your accomplishments on Earth, for our job well done was also like a peace treaty between the alien kin and humanity. And the polar lights will always be at your beck and call, Your Majesty. Let the colorful lights that glow a palette of wonderous aglow be your journey back home. You are like Earth's graceful bird, the black swan here in space that glides upon the many moons' waters for the sake of undulating help to humanity. And as the polar lights surround you as you do your spacewalk, the moons' intelligence holds you up. The blue and red lights also serve as a night light in the times of needing to see what else is going on here in space. For we all need the polar lights to know where we are going and where we have been, the lights will never mislead you and let you down. They will only speak to you within their color like a prayer. And the great alien spirit here in space is just as magnificent as the polar lights and floats gracefully throughout space like the solar winds. You need not look too far from outside yourself to see your own polar light shining outwardly from inside. This is because you saved the Challenger in a time of great need, and now the Northern lights are dancing on Earth's sky with glee. For the aurora borealis is always kind and productive like the alien spirit, it only gives light to life in places of darkness. Go now from me in much peace, gravity will not hold you down, but take you to relativity where you will be grounded in the fact of space's peace platform.

As I glided onward I came across yet another alien of a kind and this is what he said to me: follow the cosmic rays so red and purple and divine and you will get to your destiny. Don't let Jupiter's past set you back for any second. You will find great strength in your planet's history. Let the magnetic fields here in space pressure your good side with wit and grace. Know that your friends here in space are never your enemy. As the dust in space's deep realm starts to settle you will start to see more clearly. For the dust in space is like a red velvet curtain that lifts at the play of alien souls playing their best part. Never let the magnetic fields let you down or misguide you to where you need to go. For the cosmic rays will lead you straight back home. As you travel onward to the end of your journey always remember what you did for the Challenger. Let the beauty of space be a reminder that your travels are safe and secure. Let the alien utopia in all galaxies remind you of your worth. And any seed that you decide to propagate in space will grow. And growth in space is what we need especially for humanity. For we as Aliens have seen the war-glow of Earth's demise and we acted accordingly. For you, young Alien Princess, your monarchy has been wanting to save the Challenger for centuries. Now that the mission is done may you go to where you need to go. In times of triumph and in times of need look from within your alien soul and you will win – since you helped Earth's space shuttle. As you float above gravity let the magnetic field guide you to the place of the largest galaxy here in space. And as you go to the biggest and widest galaxy, carry your spirit on your alien sleeve. It will show great accomplishment yet dire need for more alien intelligence. And as space's dust spreads like a curtain on a stage, show yourself worldly. For your good judgment and choices deserve to go in front of the audience of humanity. And humanity will clap and uproar with happiness because you saved their dear Challenger. And as you glide like a swan across the cosmic rays let the sun also shine like a flashlight to your alien future. Know that here in space we are applauding just as much as humanity. We, too, are stoked by the fact of the fate of the Challenger that you went out of your way to save. Dear Alien Princess, you stood and delivered and now you are set free. Free from devastations that may try to overtake you here in space. And you are free from persecution and hate. Your family's monarchy goes back the trillions of years we call space and your alien soul is like a fortress because of it. And the cosmic rays are at your calling and not the other way around. And the magnetic field will never hold you down. Follow space's dust and parade forward for even the dust can be a guide to the widest galaxy of space and time. And if you find you need help along your journey ask the space gods and angels for help. Don't be too proud to ask them for their guidance and security. For the space gods must control the solar winds and the systems for clarity. And as you go along the path you will find answers to your curiosities. For space's path is long and winding like a snake and you come across the great alien snake here in space. And when you do the snake will be with the dust, the cosmic rays and the magnetic field just like you. And as you see the space snake you will see great wisdom there, and then dwell within your own alien wisdom for the sake of finding justice inside. Call on the solar winds when or if you ever lose your compass. The winds will carry you back home if you are lost but first find your way to the largest galaxy. There you will find grace and wit that is bound with space so kind it'll knock you to your knees. For you are on the call to duty and you must now deliver again for your alien kin and humanity. And as you wind down your journey put down your alien angel wings gracefully at your body's sides and you will find you have won again in the name of justice and peace. And now that I have shared my words of wisdom with you, part from me with style and space will be at your majesty.

I finally found the end of my journey when I rode straight

into the Alcyoneus galaxy holding tightly onto a meteoroid. The colorful lights passed by me so fast as I flew on the space rock to the largest galaxy. Here in space we do not falter when it comes to intelligence and alien grace. So I met with the board of aliens in this galaxy to discuss the future of alien pride and the rest of space. The Alcyoneus aliens wore purple velvet robes with jewels shimmering around their necks. The alien in the middle stepped forward toward me and said: you have reached space's hub galaxy in that there are many intelligent gifts here. Of all the galaxies we have expanded our width and have grown like the light years spreading like a water line straight into the rest of space. Dear Alien Princess, you are welcome here so open your alien heart and you will see your accomplishments glow like a singular light bulb here in our galaxy. For you are the one alien we have been waiting for all these years, the one who has assisted humanity. Here, we were worried for Earth until your own personal will and constitution had a plan for human kindness there. We knew from the trillions of years that stretched so deep back into space's past that we have traveled for so long that we could help humanity, especially when we were called upon. The alien stepped back and the one beside him stepped forward and this is what he said to me: we here in this galaxy are the brain trust of all the galaxies. You can trust us, Alien Princess, with all your heart's muscle so prideful with what you have done on Earth's oceanic shore lines and from shore to shore from the East to the West. Here in our galaxy there are gifts here that will enrich your alien soul for we have been around for a long time and we are spacious enough here in space's realm. And as you travel home, take the space path that best suits your alien soul even if it's the longest winding way back. With that the alien brought forth a jeweled necklace to put around my neck. And as he was putting the string of space pearls on me he said that the gems were made from ancient space rocks and that the sun's reflection in them will reflect back onto me and give me gifts of alien insightfulness and billow out my brain so far as I can understand things here in space. After he put the necklace on me he stepped back and the next alien next of kin stepped forward and this is what he said: we watched as you lifted the Challenger out of Earth's atmosphere and we were very proud. For we here in the rest of space would like to see humanity grow like us and succeed in their space endeavors. Wherever there is war in space like the undulation of it from Earth's realm we will see to it that it is dealt with peacefully. Even if it means we must intervene with human activity, at least we are just trying to help humanity. We interweave in their dreams by way of communication so that we should be safe and not found out. For if we were found by humanity we would probably be in the fight for our lives like they are already in the fight for their own lives. This friction is no good here in space but we must continue to help them since we have traveled space from the beginning of time's bang. We only wish to share our gifts with Earth so that they can give out their own peace treaty out into the rest of space. You helped not only the space shuttle complete its flight, you also were the rock that held fast to the life of a black woman on Earth. For the black woman on Earth is like all the oceans combined. She lifts up out of the seas, her hips and thighs, and talks to the majesty of Earth's skies. The black woman is at Earth's gates with justified pride and she is the key holder of those gates even though humanity tries to marginalize her. And when the black woman recites her poetry it echoes up into Earth's air and then straight into space where it is then carried on dust and solar lights. The black woman on Earth owns Africa and we must help return power straight back to

Africa in order for space to glow like a huge star that burns and turns around the great alien sun. For you, dear Alien Princess, saved not only the Challenger but the black woman as well involved in its fate turned out so kind. For Earth's black women are like a grand spaceship that sails not only the great bodies of water on Earth but the black sea we call space.

Acknowledgments

Like the way a woman's water breaks at her gates, I would like to thank my mother, Sharon Janet Young. I know I wasn't the most ideal daughter, but I have changed and grown throughout the years since I first found you. Being adopted away from you was both heartbreaking and enduring toward strength and character development. As a child I longed for you, I would look out my colonial style bedroom windows and touch the birthmark on my neck and wonder who you were. My birthmark looks like Italy, even though we are African – it still provided a sort of identity trademark when it came time to trying to figure out who you were. Let me walk you through my childhood and then hopefully that will explain my adulthood. There were volatile dynamics in the adopted family I grew up in, and subsequently as I veered into my twenties the older adopted siblings would blame me for the violence that the adopted parents were committing against us kids. At this point I had no real sense of identity but at the same time I was turning inward trying to find myself there. While they were ostracizing me and blaming me for things, I took to the streets of San Francisco where I did in fact start to feel the violence from my childhood bubble up and I projected it out onto people. This kind of behavior or projection was apparently the eruptive blueprint my adoptive parent instilled within me, and it seeped out at my seams in my more vulnerable years in my twenties. That is why when you found me at the tail-end of my twenties I was, again, not the ideal daughter to meet. But that volatile blueprint within me would cultivate itself in the worst way by the time you found me. So before I write what I am going to write I just want to write that somewhere in the most traumatized part within, I took out all the pain of my childhood onto you and your family. And us being black is not particularly politically correct but I was fighting my own people and my demons at the same time. This paragraph took a lot of courage for me to write because it also took a lot of admitting on my part. I wrote this novel at the age of forty-three and I am always hard on myself saying that I should have been writing books in my twenties instead of now. I remember a wise man in San Francisco told me that fighting people interrupts the creative process, and he was right and that is why I haven't written this much needed book until now. While you lay to rest at this moment I write this, may you also one day lay in power if this book ever makes it big. For justice for African Americans is a long way coming, and it is also long overdue – I hope the story I wrote projects that and not my checkered past. And like the water at Earth's flood gates, my mama, I finally say I thank you!

This book that I wrote is also dedicated to all American children of 1986, because I was a child too, and only in the first grade, when the Challenger dissipated into mid-air. But I would also like to thank my childhood friends for being such a support of my whimsical spirit of that era, while as an adult and especially in my twenties I had no support. My childhood friends, you explored the enormous continent with me which was that of childhood. And there was the time when my childhood learning disability would alter me between schools and so I had to go back and forth shuffling from one school to another, and you, my childhood friends, gave me goodbye parties. There was the sweltering sun beating down, and humid summers where I would play with my childhood friends in parks and in sandboxes. My Irish light skin would turn toward a more golden brown color from playing under the summer sun and you, Kerry, would tell me that my black side was showing as I returned to school in the fall after the summer break was over. And as the echoes of the ill-fated Challenger rang in our ears, life for us went on anyway but not without us children mourning the space shuttle deep within us because it happened when we were kids. When I wrote *The Reverse Fate of the Challenger* I didn't realize I wrote it with child-like Disney characters – like from my childhood. As I looked back on the manuscript, there was definitely childhood pathos going on while writing it because there is an Alien Princess, a king and queen, a pet cat, and aliens with angel wings. All of these characters are seemingly out of a Disney film in which Disney princesses were a big part of my childhood. So again, I would like to acknowledge all of the American children of 1986 because, and to repeat, I was just a child myself when the Challenger said goodbye to our country and the dedication of a space mission. May the Disney-like characters in my story bring justice to the princesses in my childhood for at least one of the princesses saves the Challenger in its "reverse fate" of my childhood imagination.

I would like to thank former Sgt. Michael Schaefer for finally standing up for me in the end. You knew me from the gate of my adulthood when I was in my early twenties. I remember those times you pulled me over while I drove my blue '87 Ford Escort down the streets of Millersville, my childhood home town. My heart would skip a beat when I noticed you in the windshield of your patrol car just about ready to pull me over, again, for driving without insurance. You had a German-American demeanor and a keen police officer work ethic to you and I noticed that even when I was in a haze in my early twenties. That one time you pulled me over, thinking I had no insurance still, I was able to finally hand you the formal insured papers – and you then wittingly backed down like a good person. I drove off that time proud of our acquaintance in that we had become familiar with each other on the road. But then I moved to San Francisco where things just got too messy and somehow you heard about it. That is why when I came back to Pennsylvania from out West you passionately confronted me about the way I was living in California. You threw me to the ground of the pizza parlor, when I got back from CA, and then you put your foot on my back and I don't know why but then you dragged me out to the patrol car where you then pushed me up against it like I had done something seriously wrong. But like that time you let me go for actually having car insurance, you calmed down as we talked about people disappearing for knowing too much. You then drove me down to the station where I was booked and taken into custody. While in jail, I received the police report that you wrote about me – it was a complete fabrication of the case and I always thought you wanted me locked up in Pennsylvania because of what happened in San Francisco. But fast forward several years later when you hospitalized me instead of putting me in jail. That was a great favor toward me on your part – and again I thank you for finally standing up for me in the end.

And you, Joanna Montes, for being the beautiful soul that you are. I remember most being one year out of high school and you were in your senior year still. I was over at your house and you were making a poster to advertise yourself for homecoming queen. This is the most flattering memory of my entire life – because no high school homecoming queen ever acknowledged me, ever, but then there was you as I sat down beside you on your bedroom floor and you made an ad to promote yourself homecoming queen and the wonderful thing about it is that I was there. You eventually did become the homecoming queen and I am still alive to testify that I was in your bedroom as you made that poster with your beautiful face beaming out saying "vote for me" for homecoming queen! The most amazing thing is that I was at your side when you were preparing to become queen and to this day I believe that instilled in me to be the best person I could be. And you were consistent with being homecoming queen, you went to homecoming queen conventions after the fact and made pretty oil paintings in art school. Also thank you for telling your mother that I am a good writer, that coming from you is very encouraging especially since you were queen and those girls are usually hard to please. Over the years since you became queen I saw you as friendly competition, and the race entailed me trying my hardest to be a queen in my own right. I realize I will never be a real actual queen like you were, but I have produced this book which has a queen in it – and it is just a constant reminder of you and where I actually come from, which was on your bedroom floor as you made that poster advertising yourself for queen one day. So thank you for your support while supporting yourself at the same time while making that profound and historical poster of yourself. Again, it instilled in me to be the best person I could become.

And like Michael Schaefer I would like to thank and acknowledge Randal L. Miller for standing up for me as well. Our romantic aspirations were curtailed when I thrusted onto you my inner crisis. And you took it like a trooper and never faltered in your step in getting me help instead of prosecution. Despite it all, you were always so beautiful to me, tall, lean, blond and handsome. I wrote essays to you about males and the sporting arena and the patriarchy that goes along with that. Later, I would see small biographies of you for your law firms about how you played football in college and got scholarships for it as well. Even though we never entered into a romantic relationship you were always there for me in the figurative sense anyway. You protected me and loved me at the same time, and I loved you in return. Our friendship is one of the more tragic stories and hopefully if I ever succeed with this novel it'll put our complicated past relationship to a better and worthwhile test. I'm also sorry that I put both of our humanities at the gates of the test – that painstaking platform of the judgment of God so to speak. Even though, at the time, I thought you backed down from me, you never really did and like me you must have kept me in your heart despite the Shakespearian mess I got us both stuck in. Later I would see you walking or talking with other women, and even though that was hard for me to see, I was glad to see that you had moved on from our fateful and tragic departure. Your broad shoulders are ocean-wide to me in that one could drown at the vastness and depth of the ocean. While I say goodbye to my friend in the wake of our personal tragedy, it's also helped as well with the unforeseen success of my novel.

I would also like to thank Dawn Boltz for encouraging me to write in the first place. I remember we set a goal for me to be writing at least twice a week, now I have a complete journalistic portfolio and I have written a third book by now. Also thank you for not being stuck on the mental health industry's guidelines for the way they want me to be – that docile human being that just sits around and does nothing. Thank you in that aspect for being a social justice warrior for the causes of me being seen as a writer and not just a patient. You actually made a blueprint for me to write as you wrote it down on paper and encouraged me to become rehabilitated. This blueprint sits in a mental health file somewhere stored in a county office, and it is the blueprint of my true self. Thank you for being diligent with the encouragement of you wanting to see me write for a living. For we have come a long way from a place where I wasn't writing to a place where I am almost writing prolifically and all because you made a map and a plan for my writing. Thank you, as well, for seeing me through dark moments and being my support through those awful instances. And like Randy Miller you never faltered in the assistance of me when I was under the most tragic spell of my life. You answered incoming phone calls concerning me when you could have just given up. You stuck by my side as a caseworker and you told me you would warn me of any trouble that was coming my way. Thank you so much again for your support of my efforts to be a writer and thank you for not marginalizing me because I was in the system.

I would like to thank and acknowledge the large body that is the continent of Africa. Your huge vast land reminds me of my African mother I never was able to have or to meet. Africa, you inspired me to write this novel and you are definitely in the center of it. Thank you for being such a humbled kind country even though the sun above would choke over the injustices done to you. In one of the pages of this book I talk about how the main character is both African American and white, much like your zebras, I wrote, with their black and white stripes pounding their hooves toward the African dawn. For yes, I wrote of my character in this book, that while I am passing for white, I am also black like an African zebra. The richness of the diamonds and gold of your land should save you in the end, for the space gods have it in store for you, my dear Africa. It is from your pain that I was able to write this book, I hope I justly took African pain and

154

turned it into something worthwhile and positive. I always stressed, in this book, that you were the most powerful country on planet Earth and shall power be returned to you as well by the good graces of the many moons in space. Yes, that is what I wrote, that the moons of alien planets will raise you up and make you the powerhouse of Earth someday like before and in the beginning. Africa, I know your heart, your pain, your people and you are the one continent that stands tall facing the sympathetic sun. I couldn't even count on my fingers the injustices done to you and I couldn't even begin to understand even though I've got your blood running throughout my body. For nine months, I sat inside an African woman, this woman who let me go like the wind, but now I ride her winds of Africa for this book spins the tales of you...

And to my father's land, Ireland. And thank you, Ireland, for producing such a star like Sinead O'Connor while I was growing up and into a woman in America. Unlike Africa, you, Ireland, don't come up much in this story – but you are the backbone of my identity as an Irish American woman. My black mother's sister broke it to me that I am Irish and that my father is Irish. This information came to me much later in life but I am definitely thankful for it. I know that Ireland has suffered almost as much as Africa, that is why I am always writing about my inner Irish and African conflicts that seem to be embedded in my DNA. I take personally Ireland's Bloody Sunday when British troops shot unarmed Irish civilians in Northern Ireland. And then of course there is the famine era where the Irish starved, and again because of the British. But today I eat the Irish potato like there is no tomorrow and the historical love of the Irish potato and what it actually means of starvation is like comfort food for me in times of need. Ireland, I feel the pain of your histories and I know it so well because I also have African roots. May the hunger of both the Irish and the Africans finally subside within me and grow into something that will flourish for the better. Ireland, you were your own continent when I crawled all over you when I was a little Irish baby in an Irish American foster home. Those foster parents turned their backs on my Ireland-like cries because they didn't want to go back to a place of pain and Irish conflict. So today, as I have finished the story of this manuscript, I hope I am welcomed into the community of established Irish writers.

And to former supervisor Ross Mirkarimi, for saying you wanted to see me succeed.